THE DOCTOR FALLS IN LOVE

Rona Randall

Chivers Press • G.K. Hall & Co.
Bath, England   Thorndike, Maine USA

This Large Print edition is published by Chivers Press, England, and by G.K. Hall & Co., USA.

Published in 2001 in the U.K. by arrangement with the author, c/o Juliet Burton Literary Agency.

Published in 2000 in the U.S. by arrangement with Juliet Burton Literary Agency.

U.K. Hardcover   ISBN 0-7540-4289-8   (Chivers Large Print)
U.K. Softcover   ISBN 0-7540-4290-1   (Camden Large Print)
U.S. Softcover   ISBN 0-7838-9191-1   (Nightingale Series Edition)

The text of this Large Print edition is unabridged.
Other aspects of the book may vary from the original edition.

Set in 16 pt. New Times Roman.

Printed in Great Britain on acid-free paper.

British Library Cataloguing in Publication Data available

Library of Congress Cataloging-in-Publication Data

Randall, Rona, 1911–
    The doctor falls in love / Rona Randall.
        p. cm.
    ISBN 0-7838-9191-1 (lg. print : sc : alk. paper)
    1. Physicians—Fiction. 2. Riviera (France)—Fiction.
    3. Large type books.   I. Title.
    PR6035.A58 D6 2000
    823'.912—dc21   00–058179

CHAPTER ONE

The letter came when John was leaving his surgery. He met the postman at the gate, took the little pile of letters, and thrust them on to the dashboard shelf indifferently. So he didn't see Catherine's handwriting staring up at him from the envelope, like a voice from the past. Not until he had driven into Monte Carlo, met Susan Lorrimer, and concluded his business with her.

He found the Villa d'Este easily enough. It was a pleasant house off the Boulevard des Moulins and proudly called itself a private hotel. A middle-aged woman sat behind a reception desk; grey-haired, plump, and maternal. When he asked for Susan Lorrimer she answered amiably:

'I'm afraid my daughter is out. She shouldn't be long. Would you care to wait?'

He took a seat in the attractive lounge hall; English in atmosphere and furnishing. An old lady sitting opposite observed him with bright, bird-like eyes. There was both curiosity and speculation in her glance, which rather amused him. She was tiny, withered, and as alive as an electric needle. Her hands flew swiftly over her sewing.

It wasn't long before a girl came through the front door, carrying a portable typewriter. Mrs.

1

Lorrimer spoke to her, indicating John with a glance, and the girl put down her typewriter and came towards him.

She was an ordinary sort of girl; he didn't notice her much, as a person. She wore a simple cotton dress and her hair was short and almost straight. She wasn't pretty, either; just pleasant, like her mother, in an ordinary sort of way.

'You wish to see me?' she asked.

He rose and extended his hand.

'My name's Curtis—John Curtis. I hear you do typing for people . . .'

'Part-time only. You see, I help mother here at the hotel.'

He smiled. 'Part-time is all I want. To be honest, it's all I can afford as yet. I run a clinic out at the village of St. Maria—a clinic for sick children.'

Interest showed in her face.

'Could you fit in occasional work there with your other commitments, Miss Lorrimer?'

'How often would you need me?'

'Two or three mornings, or afternoons, a week. More, later, I hope. My clinic is small as yet, but naturally I hope to expand. It isn't easy to get established in a foreign country.'

She didn't ask why he chose to work in a country other than his own. In a way, he was glad about that.

They agreed upon terms and that she should come to the clinic the following

2

afternoon.

Susan watched his tall figure stride out into the Riviera sunlight. He was an interesting man, she thought, although in their brief interview they had exchanged no more than a few words. Nevertheless, in that time she had noticed a lot about him—his intelligent eyes, set beneath a broad forehead, from which the hair grew back in sharply defined wings. At the temples there was a sprinkling of premature greyness, a touch which added distinction to an already interesting face. The nose was aquiline, with a proud and almost arrogant definition of the bridge, and the mouth was firm—again with a suggestion of pride about it which in no way detracted from its sensitivity.

She observed his hands, too—briefly, but indelibly—because they were strong and well formed and, again, sensitive. Hands which would possess a deft and sure touch. And a gentle one.

She was surprised that she had noticed so much in so short a time and that she had done so unconsciously, with the swift precision of a mental photographic lens, but there was something different about this man; something arresting. He could never be overlooked.

An excited voice behind her said: 'Why, dear, wasn't that young Doctor Curtis—the Englishman who runs the children's clinic at St. Maria?'

Susan turned and looked at the old lady

who had watched John with such undisguised interest. Charlotte Fothergill was their most garrulous guest; inquisitive, gossipy, sometimes amusing, but often irritating. All the same, they couldn't do without her. She was a permanent guest and paid well. Besides that, Susan and her mother were genuinely fond of the old lady.

Susan had come to the Riviera with her parents a few years earlier. Joseph Lorrimer, her father, had been an artist, well known when in his prime, but gradually impoverished, as the years went by, through ill-health. Finally, they had bought the Villa d'Este with their savings and here Joseph had ended his life, painting when able, selling a few pictures when fortunate, but happy and at peace. When he died, Ruth Lorrimer, with typical courage, had continued to run the Villa d'Este as a private hotel for English visitors.

It hadn't been easy, of course. As a new enterprise, it grew slowly and with maximum effort, but the villa was conveniently situated for the shops, casino, and harbour, and Ruth Lorrimer had a sure touch when it came to home-making. Visitors to the Villa d'Este were the kind who appreciated an intimate and friendly atmosphere. Most of the guests returned and, as a result of personal recommendation, its reputation was beginning to flourish.

But this wasn't the life Ruth wanted for her

daughter—a life lacking the gaiety and normal social round which most girls of Susan's age took for granted. Susan worked hard, both at the hotel and at her typewriter. She did both ungrudgingly and well, putting in longer hours than a normal job would have demanded and doing so without complaint.

Susan was conscious of a quickening of excitement at the thought of working for John Curtis. Most of her outside employment was in commercial organisations or the British Consulate. A medical clinic was new and fascinating territory and, if all the rumours one heard in Monte Carlo were correct (and the place was always alive with rumour and gossip and speculation) this young doctor was doing a fine job out at St. Maria; a pioneering job in which it would be exciting to take part.

As for John, he forgot about the girl as he drove back up the Moyenne Corniche. He felt satisfied that he would have help with the manuscript of his book and there his interest in Susan Lorrimer ceased. The book was important to him; a record of his experiments in the field of research. He worked on it at odd hours. In the night; in between sessions at the clinic; at every available spare moment. There were no other interests in his life now.

Like Susan's parents with their home, he had put everything he possessed into this clinic, buying a rather dilapidated villa— cheap, because of its condition—and spending the rest of his savings, coupled with Aunt Agatha's legacy, upon equipping it with the main necessities. It had given him a fresh start in life at a time when he badly needed it.

It wasn't until he parked the car that he remembered the letters on the dashboard shelf. He glanced at them idly as he went indoors and it was then that he saw Catherine's handwriting and recognised it, even after all this time, with a sense of shock.

He couldn't open the letter immediately. He stared at it for a disbelieving moment and then went into the little room he used as an office, and shut the door. His hands didn't tremble as he tore the envelope. Experience had taught him self-control.

'*My dear John,*' he read, '*you will be surprised to hear from me, I know, but not displeased, I hope. What I have to tell you must keep until we meet, which, I hope, will be soon. I'm catching the plane to Nice tomorrow morning; I'll spend a night there and continue to Monte Carlo the next day. That will be Thursday. Will you meet me at the café opposite the Casino—the one where we used to dine together? I'll be sitting at a table outside at about three o'clock. Please be kind, and come. It's important that I see you.*'

And she finished, ironically: '*As always, Catherine.*'

As always—what? As the woman he loved? The woman who had given him up for his best friend? Not that he couldn't forgive her that,

6

of course. Reason or loyalty cannot control the heart, but for how long had she and Peter been in love without his knowledge? For quite a time, apparently. They had neither of them wished to hurt him by revealing the truth.

But all that was in the past. Catherine, too, was in the past. Or so he had thought. Yet now she was preparing to walk back into his life, just as if nothing had happened.

He thrust the letter into his pocket and there it remained for the rest of the morning, but he couldn't forget it. Even as he worked, it echoed in his mind. He ought to ignore it, of course—if he had any sense, he would. He told himself that a thousand times. But he had never had a great deal of sense where Catherine was concerned; besides, if he didn't go to meet her, she could easily trace him. She could come here, to the clinic, and probably would . . .

Today was Thursday, which meant that she'd be in Monte Carlo this afternoon. So for the second time he drove there, but this time to the Café de Paris, where he had met Catherine at every spare moment during that unforgettable holiday . . .

She was sitting at their usual table, as if in reminder—if reminder were needed—looking as lovely as ever. She was even wearing the little black suit he had liked her in so much. That surprised him. Catherine had always been fond of clothes and replenished her

7

wardrobe frequently. It was two years since he had seen her and the black suit also belonged to the past.

She hadn't changed at all; still elegant, still striking. Sitting there with the façade of the Casino in the background she looked like a particularly elegant fashion model from one of the glossy magazines.

She greeted him with her warm smile and held out both hands.

'John—it's lovely to see you!'

He found himself echoing her greeting, although, in his heart, he could not mean it. It seemed ridiculous to be exchanging politenesses with someone to whom he had once been so close.

'It seems like old times, doesn't it, John? We dined here—remember?—the first time you ever took me out.'

'I remember, Catherine . . .'

'Your aunt didn't approve, I think.'

'Aunt Agatha?' he echoed in surprise. 'She said nothing.'

Catherine laughed.

'She wouldn't! All the same, she didn't like me—the old martinet!'

That jarred a little. After all, he owed a great deal to Aunt Agatha. If it hadn't been for the legacy she left him, to add to his savings, he would never have had his clinic.

Catherine changed the subject abruptly.

'I hear you've been doing great things,

John.'

'I can't imagine where you heard that.'

For answer, she opened her handbag—and again recognition disturbed him, for it was a handbag he himself had given her as a gift. That was a rather hurtful reminder and he wondered whether it had been deliberate, or even necessary . . .

She took a newspaper cutting from the bag and handed it to him.

'Perhaps you haven't seen this, John—it was only published this week.'

To his surprise, he saw his own face looking up at him. There were other photographs, too; of the clinic and the village of St. Maria; of some of the children he was treating.

'Good publicity,' said Catherine with a smile. 'I thought, in the old days, you frowned upon it.'

'In the old days,' he answered wryly, 'I was doing nothing to merit it. I was a mere house surgeon—remember?'

She ignored the bitterness in his voice.

'But now you're doing great things, John. That article says so.'

He scanned it with interest.

'I remember, now—this journalist was passing through St. Maria to cover the Royal Wedding last spring. He spent a night in the village and there, I imagine, heard about the clinic. He paid a surprise visit before moving on next day, and even promised to write it up.

I didn't really think he would. It's decent of him and I certainly hope it will help, but he seems to have praised me rather fulsomely.'

He folded the newspaper cutting and Catherine held out her hand for it.

'May I keep it, please, John? It's precious to me . . .'

'I can't think why,' he answered indifferently, but handed it back, all the same.

'Don't be bitter, John,' she pleaded.

Their coffee came, interrupting further conversation. When the waiter had withdrawn, John said abruptly: 'You said you wanted to see me about something important. What was it?'

'Why—that! The article I've just shown you!'

'I don't understand . . .'

'It says you're short of staff.'

'Short of other things, besides. Equipment; backing. But I manage.'

'You'd manage better if you had help.'

He sat very still. Surely, she couldn't mean—?

As if reading his thoughts, she nodded.

'Yes. I do, John. I'm a nurse. Remember?'

'You are also,' he said briskly, 'a married woman. What has your husband to say about this?'

'He doesn't know—yet.'

She leaned towards him urgently and he noticed then that her eyes were not only tired, but anxious. He noticed other things, too. A small repair on the collar of her blouse; a darn in the first finger of her right hand glove; even a shininess at the elbows of her jacket. It had never been necessary for Catherine to make-do-and-mend . . .

Wasn't Peter doing too well, then? But he'd joined up with Stephen Foster in Harley Street, so he ought to be.

John said briskly: 'Catherine, I don't understand why you're here. Come to the point, will you?'

She saw that it was no use appealing to sentiment. He had steeled his heart against her. She took comfort from the reflection that if it were necessary for him to steel his heart against her, he must be afraid of her. That was pleasing. It suggested that he was still vulnerable where she was concerned.

'Do you see the English newspapers, John?'

'Not very often. When they do arrive they're a few days old and I'm much too busy to spare time for anything but medical journals these days.'

'Then, if you haven't seen the papers, of course you don't know, but I should think you must be the only member of the medical profession who doesn't.' She paused, then finished abruptly: 'Stephen Foster's name is to be crossed off the medical register.'

CHAPTER TWO

For a long moment Catherine returned John's stare, then, when he failed to answer, she continued: 'Of course, it may not surprise you. You never had a good opinion of him— naturally.'

She didn't glance at his hand, but he knew she was remembering a scalpel shaking in fingers unnerved by alcohol, and his own flashing forward, seizing the instrument before it could reach the unconscious form on the operating table, and the scalpel slipping . . . severing his own wrist . . .

No, he had never had a good opinion of Stephen Foster even before it happened.

He said coldly: 'Have you come here to plead for him—to me?'

'No,' she answered quietly. 'For Peter.'

'Peter!'

'He will suffer almost as badly. Wherever he goes, people will say: "Don't you remember— he was mixed up with that man called Foster?" Apart from being Stephen's partner, he had nothing to do with the affair, of course. It's a cheap little story, I'm afraid. The newspapers called it "exceeding his duties as a doctor with a well-known débutante". That's putting it politely. Of course, doctors are fair game for lies and scandal and in this case the girl

12

pursued Stephen brazenly. Possibly he enjoyed her adoration, but he's certainly had to pay for it. The damages were heavy enough to ruin him financially, let alone professionally. Oh, it isn't Stephen I care about—it's Peter. Look at this!'

She thrust a folded newspaper before him. Headlines glared—sordid and unpleasant. There was a photograph of a rather glamorous girl and another of Stephen Foster. Beneath it, also, was one of Peter. It was a good likeness. His pleasant, rather weak, face looked out from the printed page. There was a caption beneath.

'Peter Collier, partner to the guilty man.'

Catherine said furiously: 'Why they had to drag Peter's name in, I can't imagine! He wasn't involved in any way.'

'The newspaper admits that. All it really says about Peter is that he was prominent in and around Harley Street . . .'

Wasn't that what Catherine had wanted—a husband well known in the West End? He thrust the thought aside. Bygones were bygones and it was more than two years since Catherine had broken her engagement to himself because of his refusal to join with Stephen Foster in Harley Street. As if he would have anything to do with a man like that, after the hospital incident! So Peter had joined with him instead—at Catherine's instigation, no doubt. Peter had once been

13

John's friend and the fact that they had both loved the same woman was no reason for hating him now. The fact that he had been so unwise as to join up with the wrong man was no reason for despising him, either.

John said: 'Surely, Peter can start on his own again?'

'That needs money,' Catherine answered abruptly. 'We haven't any. That surprises you, doesn't it? It surprises me, too. I had no idea how expensive life in Harley Street could be! We lived up to every penny. Entertaining. Putting on a show. Being seen at the right places, at the right time, with the right people. It was Stephen's idea, of course, and all with the aim of widening the practice; all to publicise the names of Stephen Foster and Peter Collier! I sound bitter, don't I? Well, I am bitter. Bitter and disappointed. That is why I've come to you now—to ask you, to *beg* you, to give me a job. Peter, too.'

He answered gently: 'I'm sorry, Catherine. I simply can't afford to take on staff.'

'But Peter is worth helping! You know that. You always said he was a good doctor and you could do with a man of his ability in your clinic, obviously. You always worked well together, too. You even made plans . . .'

'You've no need to remind me of that, Catherine.'

She laid a hand upon his sleeve.

'John, you've every reason to despise me, I

14

don't blame you for that, but not Peter. Not really. In your heart, you know that. I came to plead for him—not for myself!'

The lovely tones of her voice flowed over him.

He answered gently:

'Of course I would help you both if I could, but I'm having the devil's own job to keep the clinic going as it is, even single-handed. I could pay so very little, Catherine.'

'But a little is all we'd want, or need!' She indicated the feature article about his work. 'That house looks big enough to accommodate just two more people! And we'd both be working—remember that.' She even achieved a light laugh as she finished: 'We'd earn our bread and butter, I assure you, and the jam could come later, when the clinic was flourishing!'

It was a generous offer and he appreciated it.

She knew, then, that she had won. She pressed home her advantage by adding eagerly: 'I could help in other ways, too! To save money, I've been acting as Peter's receptionist; attending to the secretarial side and things like that. I could do the same for you.'

'That won't be necessary, Catherine. I engaged a part-time girl only this morning. She starts tomorrow.'

'Then cancel the engagement!' she cried

happily.

'No. I couldn't do that. It wouldn't be fair.'

She shrugged.

'Secretaries can always get jobs these days, you know.'

He thought of Susan Lorrimer, working part-time in her mother's hotel and supplementing their income on her typewriter. He remembered the inexpensive cotton frock she wore and the plastic handbag she carried. He had heard that Mrs. Lorrimer was a widow; in fact, he had heard the whole story from the barber who came to the clinic to cut his own and the children's hair. The man visited the Villa d'Este, also, to trim some of the peppery old colonels who stayed there.

No, he couldn't reject Susan Lorrimer because Catherine was willing to serve him.

'Does Peter know you've come to see me, Catherine?'

'Of course not! He'd have forbidden it. May I write to him tonight and give him the news?'

'Please do. How soon will he be able to come?'

'Any time now,' she answered happily. 'What remains of the practice can be put in the hands of an agent. It won't fetch much, but at least it will help to tide us over until the clinic is as flourishing as you would wish.'

Before parting, they walked together on the Casino terrace, overlooking the Mediterranean.

'How blue it is!' Catherine sighed. 'I

remember the first time we stood here together—the Mediterranean was as blue as it is today.'

'It is always blue—even when the skies are grey.'

'I was holidaying alone,' she continued, 'and you were dancing attendance upon your Aunt . . .' Her eyes mocked him, but her smile was not unkind. He had never known, of course, that she had deliberately followed him here, that she had turned down a holiday in Spain, all expenses paid by her father, because she knew John was to be in Monte Carlo, and back at the hospital he never seemed to notice her . . .

'If it hadn't been for Aunt Agatha,' he said, 'I would never have had any holidays at all. She brought me up. She educated me. She left me, finally, everything she had.'

'And in return you were at her beck and call!'

'It never seemed like that to me. I was fond of her. Genuinely fond.' His voice was abrupt.

'I'm teasing, John!'

There was laughter in her eyes now; the anxiety was gone. She began to muse nostalgically: 'I'd had to pinch and scrape for that holiday myself, you know, but it was worth every penny because through it I met you. *Really* met you, I mean. Before that, you'd merely passed me with a nod in the corridors or rapped commands at me in the ward . . .'

Pinch and scrape? he thought in surprise. But Catherine's parents had been comfortably off. That was why she had dressed so well, even on a nurse's pay. They'd given her a first-class education and a 'finishing' at a select social school. It was a tribute to her character and independence that she had chosen a nursing career when it had not really been necessary for her to earn her living.

He said gently: 'Couldn't your parents have helped when things went wrong?'

She appeared to hesitate briefly, then answered with a proud tilt of her head: 'I have pride, John. I wouldn't go to them and ask for help. I'd rather come to you and ask for work.' She added ruefully: 'Besides, when I broke my engagement to you Daddy rather washed his hands of me. He was fond of you, John, and I suppose he saw what a dreadful mistake I was making.'

He said evenly: 'It is never a mistake to marry the person you love.'

She made no answer. The time was not ripe to tell him the truth. She would pick her moment for that. She gave a covert glance in his direction and thought: 'He's more attractive now than ever he was!' Was it two years' separation that made her see him through different eyes, or was it merely that responsibility had deepened his self-reliance— which, in the old days, she had come to regard as stubbornness? Whatever the cause, the

18

result was impressive. What a fool she had been to turn him down!

On the other hand, if *he* had aimed for Harley Street, as she had so passionately desired him to, he'd have got somewhere. And he'd have gone the right way about it, too. Not like Peter, following weakly in Stephen Foster's wake.

She felt the familiar surge of contempt and anger towards her husband, blaming him for the failure for which she, initially, was responsible. That was typical of Catherine. If her decisions turned out badly, others were to blame; never herself.

She continued: 'I don't mean that there was any estrangement between myself and my parents, but you know how it is when one marries—one grows away from one's people.'

He smiled a little.

'I wouldn't know. I've never been married.'

But he couldn't imagine himself growing away from Aunt Agatha, with whom he had shared a mental bond which Catherine had never been able to understand. Agatha knew of his dreams and ambitions and encouraged them. To see them grow to fruition would have made her happy. He often wished she could see the clinic at St. Maria.

Catherine continued softly: 'I remember how you confided all your plans to me, John. All your dreams. How you wanted to specialise in children's diseases . . .'

19

'And you thought I meant in the West End. You could never understand that Harley Street was not the Mecca of all doctors.'

'I understand now,' she said bitterly.

They were leaning against the stone balustrade, but now she turned her back upon the sea and concentrated her gaze upon him.

'You'll find I'm a very different person, John. I've changed.'

There was an intimate note in her voice from which he shied.

'Not in appearance, at least,' he answered lightly. 'You're as lovely as ever.'

'Do you think so? Do you *really* think so? I'm glad of that, John. I thought you might be hating me.'

She seemed to overlook the fact that it was possible to admire a person's beauty and hate them just the same, but he smiled at her frankly and said: 'To be honest, I thought I did. I've thought so for a long time ...'

'And now?

'Now I don't think so any more.'

Impulsively, she reached up, placed her hands upon his shoulders and kissed him. Not upon the lips, but upon the cheek. Even that— light and impersonal as it was—brought the old familiar surge of emotion rushing through him, so that he drew away imperceptibly, alarmed at the effect she still had upon him.

'Are you staying in Monte Carlo?' he jerked.

'I don't know. I haven't decided. Last night I

stayed in Nice. Perhaps it would be better to go back to England and tell Peter my news, but, frankly, I can't afford it.' She looked at him in the old familiar way—a swift glance from beneath her lashes. 'You may as well know the truth, John—I couldn't afford a return ticket; only the single fare and enough to tide me over.'

She had been as confident as that that he wouldn't reject her. She had always been sure of him and now in her heart she felt elated and rather proud of herself. Why had she ever feared that this man would cease to love her? Why had she been so foolish, even when her love for Peter began to wane and she paused to look back, with regret, upon the love she had discarded? It was there, all the time, waiting for her. She knew that now.

'It would have been cheaper to come by train, I know,' she continued swiftly, 'but not so quick, and when I read that article I knew what I had to do. It was just as if heaven itself had shown it to me, for a reason. So—I came. As to how I was to get back, I'm afraid I didn't think of that. The important thing was to see you, and now that I have and everything is settled, it isn't even necessary for me to return. I'll write to Peter and say he'll be hearing from you. You will confirm things with him, won't you?'

'Of course. But he might say no—have you thought of that?'

'Why should he? He hasn't a chance to get started again in any other way, but that won't be his true reason for accepting. He'd like to work with you again, John. I know that. He's always grieved over the rift between you. Stephen was a pretty poor substitute as a partner.'

'There is always one bad egg in every basket, and a bad egg in the medical profession is spotted more quickly than in any other. A man without integrity cannot hope to survive in it. Peter needn't fear that he'll suffer for Stephen Foster's reputation.'

'I know that. All the same, a fresh start away from all his old environs will be good for him. Even better will be an opportunity for reunion with you. And I'll be glad to be nursing again, believe me. I need to do something useful, something worthwhile; something to prove myself again. I wasn't really meant to be a lily-of-the-field.'

She made a pretty decorative one, all the same, his glance said—which pleased her. She continued confidently:

'Peter will be delighted to come, I assure you. The fact that you both did your training together, started together, held your first House appointment together, means a lot to him still. Beside, you tried to entice him into this clinic idea in the old days, didn't you?'

'It was a dream we had,' he admitted, 'although we hadn't thought of the Alpes-

Maritimes as a *locale.*'

'What made you?'

'I had my reasons,' he evaded. 'One being that memorable holiday—again thanks to Aunt Agatha. She wanted to visit the *perfumeries* at Grasse one day and on the way back we made a detour through St. Maria. The rarefied atmosphere convinced me that it was the ideal spot for a clinic of this type—so, when I had no one but myself to consider, I returned.'

'But Peter discarded the dream because of me—and you were alone, because of me. Oh, I know I was to blame, John, and I despise myself for it now. But I've told you that I've changed—and it's true. I've learned my lesson.'

He felt a swift pity for her. It couldn't have been easy for a girl like Catherine to have her illusions shattered.

His car was parked by the gardens in the Place du Casino and as they strolled towards it he was in a quandary as to what to do with her tonight.

'You'd better cable Peter, if you really don't intend to go back, Catherine.'

'Where's the point? It will only mean returning and that seems unnecessary expense to me. We just can't afford it, my dear. All Peter need do is pack his bags and come. Everything we leave behind can be sold. Anything I particularly want, he can bring, but there's nothing I'd break my heart over losing.'

She looked up at him and said bitterly: 'Pretty, isn't it?'

'It is—unfortunate,' he answered carefully, 'but you can both make a fresh start here and forget the past.'

'And you? Can you forget the past, too?' she asked quietly.

'I have already forgotten it,' he lied.

She dropped his arm and didn't speak again until they reached his car.

'John—will you take me back to St. Maria with you? Couldn't I wait for Peter there?'

It was this very idea which he'd been trying to suppress, hoping she wouldn't think of it. It seemed the obvious solution, of course, but he'd have to think of some excuse to reject it. Seeing her again this afternoon was enough of an upheaval for one day; to have her living beneath the same roof, alone, even for a brief time, would be intolerable. And but for his housekeeper and the clinical staff they would, virtually be alone. She would be his guest until her husband arrived and he would, of course, have to entertain her, dine with her, live in a proximity he did not care to contemplate.

He said at random: 'I'm afraid it isn't practical, Catherine. Rooms will have to be prepared. My housekeeper warned. But I know of a nice little hotel I can take you to, run by an English woman, for English people, and I'm sure you'll be comfortable there.'

And so he took her to the Villa d'Este.

CHAPTER THREE

Susan was carrying old Mrs. Fothergill's tray of tea across the lounge when John and Catherine entered and, like the rest of the occupants, she viewed their arrival with interest.

She placed the tray before the old lady and went across to the reception desk. Her mother was upstairs in the linen room. As Susan approached, John turned and smiled, saying to Catherine: 'This is Miss Lorrimer, who is coming to the clinic to work for me.'

'The part-time secretary?'

Catherine's voice held interest and she eyed Susan in a way through which any woman could see; assessing, curious, critical. Finally she rejected her. The girl smiled inwardly. She knew well enough that she was not sufficiently spectacular to rival anyone so lovely as this.

John introduced them and asked if there was a single room available for Mrs. Collier.

So she was married . . . Illogically, Susan was glad of that.

'We have a very modest one at the back of the hotel,' she said doubtfully. 'I don't know whether it would be suitable . . .'

To her surprise the woman accepted it without indulging in the continental custom of inspecting the room before doing so. Did she jump at it because it was modest and, therefore, inexpensive? She didn't look impoverished—on the contrary. Susan had become adept at judging people's means and young Mrs. Collier had an air of luxury about her, as if accustomed to only the best.

'I'll take you up, Madame. Pierre will see to your bags.' Susan signalled to the aged porter, but to her surprise Catherine said: 'I have only this one.' It was a small overnight bag, light enough to carry.

John took his departure then.

'Let me know when you hear from Peter, Catherine. Meanwhile, I'll have rooms prepared at the clinic.' He thought of three top rooms, unused as yet. They'd make a good flat for the pair of them and, that way, he need see little of Catherine except in the course of work.

'But surely I can come and help right away! Please, John—I can't just kick my heels in Monte Carlo until Peter arrives.' She saw Susan waiting at the foot of the stairs and said impulsively: 'That girl will be coming to work for you, won't she?' Tomorrow, didn't you say? I'll come with her.'

Without giving him time to answer she reached up, kissed him, and followed Susan upstairs.

Old Charlotte Fothergill's eyes followed the newcomer with speculation and delight. They hadn't had anyone so interesting at the Villa d'Este for a long time—not since that respectable married couple from Birmingham who turned out to be neither respectable nor married. Life had been rather dull since then.

The old lady's eyes became agog with curiosity. When the two girls had vanished upstairs and the doctor out into the street, she shuffled across to the reception desk and examined the new visitor's immigration form, which Susan had put aside. That was no deterrent to Charlotte, who knew, by now, just where to place her hands upon everything.

Age had not dulled Charlotte's wits—nor her eyesight. She scanned the form swiftly, taking in every detail. So, the girl was married, eh? And kissing a man who wasn't her husband! This promised to be interesting. And where did she come from? London, of course. Harley Street, indeed!

There wasn't time for more. Susan's footsteps sounded at the top of the stairs. Fortunately, the staircase curved and by the time she was in view of the lounge the old lady had reached her chair again. She was even sipping tea as if, for the past few minutes, she had done nothing else.

'Well?' she croaked. 'And did she turn her pretty nose up at the modest back room?'

'On the contrary, she liked it.'

'"Curiouser and curiouser," as Alice said! Why should a smart young Londoner be content with a room only kept for emergency bookings?'

'How did you know she was from London?' Susan asked swiftly.

'By her accent, of course,' Charlotte answered blandly. *(Oh, no, you don't catch me out, my girl!)* Besides, London is stamped all over her . . .'

Susan glanced at the tray in which she placed the registration forms prior to filing. They appeared to be just as she left them, but, of course, anyone with Charlotte's sharp eyes needn't pick one up to read . . . She made a mental note to find another place for them— not for the first time. Evading the old woman's curiosity had become a continual game of hide-and-seek.

'Well?' Charlotte rasped. 'And what do *you* think of her?'

'I think her both charming and attractive.'

'Colourful, I'll admit. So are those geraniums in the window boxes outside. Personally, I never cared for geraniums. They've a nasty sour smell. I should think Mrs. Collier could be sour, too, if it pleased her.'

'So you know her name? That means you've been snooping!'

Charlotte looked hurt.

'I don't know how you can suggest such a thing, my dear! I heard Doctor Curtis introduce her—didn't he call her Mrs. Collier?'

Susan laughed. She had to. Old Charlotte

Fothergill was never caught napping.

'Your English newspapers have come,' she said, deliberately changing the subject. 'Didn't Pierre give them to you?'

'If that is a hint to mind my own business, Susan, you're wasting your time. I've no business to mind. I'm a lonely old woman with nothing to do in life but sew—and no one to sew for, anyway. Don't deny me the pleasure of studying people, my dear. It's fun to speculate about them, even if I'm wrong. Not that I ever am, of course. Didn't I *tell* you that pair from Birmingham weren't all they seemed?'

Susan's heart softened.

'You're a wicked woman, Charlotte, but we love you. All the same, I can't stay here gossiping. Mrs. Collier wants some tea in her room.'

Returning through the lounge a few minutes later, carrying Catherine's tray, Susan saw with relief that Charlotte was deep in her pile of newspapers. That would keep her occupied for quite a time, thank goodness, even if it meant listening to snippets of scandal for days afterwards . . .

Catherine had changed into an uncrushable silk housecoat when Susan returned upstairs. The black suit was on a hanger and she was brushing it carefully. Something in the way she did it made Susan feel that she was sick of the garment and only cared for it from sheer necessity.

If I had a suit like that, thought Susan, I'd care for it for ever. It was obviously a model.

With a negligent gesture, Catherine indicated a small table beneath the window.

'I'll have it there—not that the view is particularly inspiring! A pity you hadn't a room with a view of the sea . . .'

'We keep this room for last-minute visitors, such as yourself. If you don't care for it you can, of course, give it up.'

Susan's voice was polite, but firm. Catherine viewed her in surprise. So the girl wasn't without spirit, despite her unimpressive appearance. Catherine studied her quiet face dispassionately. It was, in its way, quite pretty, but not the type to represent any sort of competition—which was a good thing since they were both to work for John. Luckily, Susan Lorrimer would only be at the clinic part-time, whereas she herself would be on the spot constantly—even with Peter around. And *he* needn't make any difference.

Catherine could be charming when she chose to be, and she chose to be right now. She smiled at Susan and answered pleasantly: 'My dear, don't misunderstand! The room will tide me over quite well until I move to St. Maria . . .'

'You're going to live there? In the village?'

'Oh, dear me, no! At Doctor Curtis's clinic. I'm a nurse.'

'I see.'

'Doctor Curtis asked me to join him. We are—old friends.'

She put a world of meaning into the last two words.

'How nice,' Susan answered inadequately, and moved towards the door.

'Don't go—stay and talk to me. It's nice to meet a compatriot abroad.'

'I'm on duty at the reception desk . . .'

Catherine waved that aside.

'If this is your "reserve" room it can't be let to anyone else, so you won't miss any business by staying here for a minute or two. I hear you're going to work for Dr. Curtis. That will be nice—we'll see more of each other, and until I move there we can travel to St. Maria together. How do we get there?'

'By autobus from the corner.'

'Tell me—what have you heard about Doctor Curtis?'

'Only that he is doing a good job out at St. Maria, but I expect a clinic of that kind is uphill work.'

'Oh, John's a climber, believe me. Cast him down and he'll get up again. He's got courage—and he's certainly needed it.'

'Why?' Susan asked, against her will. She didn't want to talk to this young woman, charming as she was. Instinct made her wary.

'He was going in for surgery—once upon a time.'

'Many doctors start as House Surgeons and

31

then branch off into medicine.'

Catherine looked at her shrewdly. So—she was a loyal little soul, eh? Well, I can be loyal, too. Loyal to John, at least. And that accident to his hand wasn't the only reason for abandoning surgery, as well as I know. Who, but I, did he confide his dreams to, long ago?

'I only meant,' she said smoothly, 'that he has needed courage to start an experimental clinic, right from scratch, in a part of the world where he was completely unknown.'

'Others have done such things. Fine men like Albert Schweitzer, for instance. I should think Doctor Curtis has something of the same crusading quality.'

Good heavens! thought Catherine with a sense of shock. *The girl's half in love with him already! I can tell from her eyes and the tone of her voice . . .*

For a brief moment they eyed each other like antagonists.

'You don't need to tell me how fine a man Doctor Curtis is,' Catherine said slowly. 'I know him—intimately. In fact, we mean a lot to one another. We always have and we always will.'

There seemed to be a strong significance in her voice. Susan pondered upon it as she went downstairs, aware of doubt and misgiving and an obscure sense of fear. Nor was it lessened by her contact with Charlotte at the foot of the stairs.

32

The old lady regarded her triumphantly.

'I knew it!' she cried. 'I *knew* there was something strange about that woman's arrival! And only one bag with her, too—that means she left in a hurry. A funny business, Susan dear, you mark my words!'

'I don't know what you are talking about.'

'But you will. You wait and see! That young woman's husband will be the next arrival, and an unsavoury couple they are, if you ask me! As for young Doctor Curtis, if he wants that clinic of his to succeed he'd better be careful with whom he associates. Mud sticks—even other people's mud. But I'm not telling you what I know—yet.'

CHAPTER FOUR

Susan paid little heed to old Mrs. Fothergill's chatter. The woman always had some tit-bit of gossip with which to regale the nearest listener and, more often than not, was totally wide of the truth. All the same, Susan's interest in John Curtis deepened and with it grew a sense of unrest.

On the whole, Susan was a practical girl. Like her mother, she had to be. There was little time for dreaming in hotel life. The day began early and finished only when the last guest had retired for the night. As yet, the staff Ruth employed was small—two chambermaids, old Pierre the porter, and kitchen staff. The management was entirely in her own capable hands, in addition to which she supervised the preparation of meals and planned all menus. Susan's help at the reception desk was therefore essential and the girl had been trained by her mother to be practical and efficient.

Nevertheless, a measure of her father's temperament was inherent in her. Besides being artistic Joseph Lorrimer had been intuitive, and this quality was sometimes apparent in his daughter. It troubled Susan now as old Charlotte turned her back, and, carrying her bundle of British newspapers, marched upstairs.

Of course, everything the woman said was nonsense and the best thing to do was to dismiss every word of it. How could she know anything about Catherine Collier *or* her husband? Besides, John Curtis wasn't the type of man to have doubtful friends. Susan judged him to be straightforward and much too intelligent to be taken in by people; also too conscientious as a doctor to risk his reputation or his work by becoming involved with anyone likely to undermine it. So all that talk about Mrs. Collier and her husband being 'unsavoury' was ridiculous and unfounded and just another sample of Charlotte's distorted imagination.

It was a pity about Charlotte, thought Susan. Time hung heavily on the old lady's hands. She was alone in the world, with no financial worries—and no friends. So what was happening to her was the too-frequent fate of many elderly women in similar circumstances; she was obsessed with the lives of others, avid for scandal, feeding her imagination with tit-bits from the gossip columns. She was pathetic, lonely, and likeable.

As Susan returned to her desk she resolved to think no more about young Doctor Curtis or the disturbing Catherine Collier. She had no grounds for feeling apprehensive about the woman and absolutely no grounds for jealousy—so why, when she thought of her, should she feel a strange little current of dislike and a fear that what Catherine hinted about her relationship with John Curtis should be not only true, but somehow dangerous to him?

It was at that precise moment that the front door of the hotel swung open and a young man strode in. Susan's face lit up at the sight of him. No one could have been more welcome than Pierre Dupont at this moment. He brought a breath of frank young manhood into the place, a practical vigour in the face of which no fancies or restless imaginings could survive.

'Suzanne, *ma petite*! I come to carry you off for a swim! No refusals, no excuses! I see your dear *maman* myself and tell her so!' And with a wide, disarming grin he marched towards the kitchen.

Ruth looked up with a smile as he entered. So did the entire kitchen staff. Everyone at the Villa d'Este knew Pierre Dupont and fully expected him to marry Susan in due course. Sometimes Ruth imagined that he expected it himself, but as to Susan's feelings, she was not quite sure. In any case, they were both too young to think of marriage yet. At least, Pierre was—not so much in years, as in character. He was twenty-three, but still a boy. Charming, good-natured, impulsive, and honest. He made no secret of his devotion to Susan, but it revealed a possessive quality which Ruth regarded as dangerous. He could be passionate and jealous—she was sure of that.

He seized her hand and kissed it with typical French gallantry. Ruth smiled.

'Don't tell me, Pierre—I know! You've come to take Susan for a game of tennis, or a swim, or a ride into Nice . . .'

'And all your protests will be useless, Madame! A day like this is too beautiful for a young girl to spend indoors. You agree—no?'

'I agree—yes! And I'm not protesting. Tell Susan I'll take over from her in five minutes.'

'Madame—no wonder you have a beautiful daughter! A nature such as yours could not fail to produce anything else!'

She laughed and gave him a friendly push

36

towards the door. 'Be off with you, Pierre, and take your flattery with you!'

'My flattery? No, madame! Your daughter? Yes!'

He was as good as his word, carrying Susan off to Monte Carlo beach on the back of his motor scooter. The wind blew through her hair as they mounted the ascending road out of Monte Carlo, and spun down towards the popular beach club. The sun was hot and as she dived into the superb swimming pool Susan felt the water close over her with a welcoming coolness. It did more than cool her physically; it obliterated the burning resentment which, illogically, had been troubling her ever since Catherine's arrival.

Afterwards, they left the pool and sun bathed upon the rocks by the sea, listening to the pounding of the surf and occasionally laughing their delight as spray deluged them. Above, on the wide terrace of the New Beach Hotel, tables were being set for afternoon tea; drowsily, Susan heard the chink of china and cutlery and the brisk feet of waiters as they set tables and deck chairs in the sun. Rolling over on to her stomach, she glanced upwards and saw the strong figure of a man standing beside the balustrade. He was silhouetted against the sky. With the sun behind him she could not discern his features, but the width and set of his shoulders were unmistakable; so, too, the shape of his head. In her brief meeting with

37

John Curtis his physical qualities had impressed her subconsciously, and she recognised them now.

She shaded her eyes with her hand, looking up at him. So he hadn't gone back to St. Maria immediately? Idly, she wondered why. If she had known he wanted tea she could have offered him some at the Villa d'Este. She regretted her lack of thought, then reflected that he would probably enjoy such a setting as this more than the chintzy atmosphere of her home.

It was a silly thought and she knew it. She rolled over on to her back again and resolved to forget him. After all, he was only a man for whom she was going to work. A new employer—nothing more. He would occupy no personal place in her life.

She heard Pierre's voice saying lazily: 'There's a man on the terrace above who is paying marked attention to you, *chérie*. I resent that.' He finished with a yawn: 'I think I will knock him down—no?'

'No,' Susan echocd sleepily.

She was stretched full length upon the flat surface of a rock, her body sheathed in a brief emerald green swim suit. Her eyes were closed, so Pierre studied her with the undisguised appreciation of the French. Normally, he tried to restrain his ardour, aware of Susan's native reserve. That, to him, was part of her charm. She didn't openly parade her physical attributes; indeed, she seemed unaware of them. Not so himself— nor, it seemed, the man above, whose attention had been focused upon her for longer than Pierre liked.

'He is impertinent, Suzanne. I think I climb these rocks and challenge him.'

'To what? A duel? Have you the energy for such activity on an afternoon like this?' Susan's voice sounded indifferent and amused.

Pierre grinned, and admitted that he had not.

He yawned again and turned his face to the sun, musing drowsily: 'Nevertheless, *chérie*, no man has any right to stare at you, but I.'

Susan made no answer. She wasn't going to pick up that cue—she knew what it would lead to. She'd been through it so often before; Pierre's possessive assurance that she was his; that no man had a right to her company but he; that no man but he should be allowed to admire her. That last thought rather amused her now. John Curtis didn't admire her in the least and wasn't likely to. He was hardly aware of her, except as someone who promised to be of use to his work.

In this, Susan was right. John had carried away from their first meeting an impression of a pleasant, ordinary sort of girl; one he liked; the type who would make a good secretary, but nothing more. Now he looked down upon her in some surprise, seeing her, for the first time as a person. And an attractive one.

Her limbs were tanned to a golden brown—a permanent shade acquired through several Riviera summers. Against the vivid green of her swimming trunks and bra the contrast was startling. Her young body was strong and well-proportioned; the doctor in him appreciated that just as the man in him appreciated the femininity of it. Susan Lorrimer had a lovely figure, a fact to which her cheap cotton frock had drawn no attention this morning. Not that he would have observed it—all he had been intent upon at that moment was fixing up his business with her and getting back to St. Maria.

He had taken advantage of this second visit to Monte Carlo to run down to the beach hotel to visit a French doctor of his acquaintance who was staying there. Periodically they met and exchanged news and views of their work. Jean Pasteur had a similar clinic in Paris and had watched John's work with interest for some time. Now, on a brief holiday, he had begged the Englishman to dine with him—an invitation John had been forced to decline owing to pressure of work. Being the only doctor at the clinic kept him bound to the place pretty consistently, but this would ease up once Peter joined him.

John felt somewhat apprehensive about the coming reunion with Peter, although eventually, he felt sure, he would be glad of it. For one thing, there would be more moments like this, when he could relax a little and think of other things besides work, and, for another, Peter's medical ambitions had once run parallel with his own. They had planned much together. Now there was the possibility that those dreams could be fulfilled.

Standing upon the terrace, overlooking the sea, John mused upon the situation as he waited for his message to be sent up to Doctor Pasteur. After depositing Catherine at the Villa d'Este he had automatically headed for home, but a restlessness had come upon him as the aftermath of their meeting and he had known a sudden desire for distraction. He didn't want to go back to his villa at St. Maria whilst the disturbance of her arrival was still fresh within him; if he did, he would spend too much time thinking and remembering and conjecturing. He wasn't sure that he had done the right thing in agreeing to her suggestion— but what else could he have done in the circumstances?

What he needed was the company of someone who would lead his mind completely away from the problem. And so he had remembered Jean Pasteur. Only a few days ago the man had driven up from Monte Carlo to visit the clinic and had tried to persuade John to spend the evening with him. That had been impossible, but an hour in the company of someone completely detached from his personal life appealed to John at this moment.

41

Whilst the reception clerk tried to trace the doctor, John had sauntered on to the terrace. He rather fancied a swim himself, and was toying with the idea of obtaining a pair of trunks at the Beach Club when his eye was caught by a girl upon the rocks below. He had a feeling that she had been watching him, although when he studied her he saw that her eyes were closed, her face upturned to the sun. He observed something more—that the young man who accompanied her was looking at her reclining figure with something more than admiration. He was plainly in love with her.

An indulgent smile touched the corners of John's mouth. The French were never ashamed of revealing their emotions and the boy made no attempt to conceal his feelings for the girl. He was young, strong, and handsome in a dark and passionate way— obviously he would make an ardent lover. For a moment John surveyed the pair with a gentle interest, touched by their youth and unselfconsciousness, then realised with an odd little sense of shock that the girl was Susan Lorrimer.

What was odd about his reaction was the surprise he felt. There was no reason for it. Nor was there any reason why she shouldn't be sunbathing upon the rocks with a handsome young Frenchman. All the same, John studied the boy with renewed observation, and it was at this moment that Pierre's lazy glance swerved upwards aad observed his interest.

John looked away, wondering if the reception clerk had succeeded in tracing Pasteur and hoping that the man would soon appear. The frank scrutiny of the young man below was embarrassing.

But it didn't last long. A moment later Susan rose, stretched herself, then dived from the rocks. Her companion followed immediately. For a time they swam neck and neck, then the boy plunged, grabbing her by the ankles and pulling her with him beneath the water. They surfaced quickly, laughing their enjoyment, and the sound struck a note of solitude in John's heart. He felt oddly alone. He watched them awhile longer, then turned his attention to the pool—more patronised than the sea owing to the jagged rocks which edged the coastline and which could catch the unwary.

At that moment the reception clerk came out of the hotel and crossed the terrace. Doctor Pasteur, he regretted, appeared to have gone out. The key to his room had been handed in and he could be found in none of the reception rooms. Perhaps M'sieu would care to leave a message?

'Only that I'll be taking a dip in the pool. If he returns before I leave, perhaps he'll join me—'

John broke off. The sound of a cry below had caught his attention. Not a loud cry, but a sharp one. Turning swiftly, he saw that Susan's companion was crouching upon a rock, half in and half out of the water. Susan had already climbed out, but now she leapt across the dividing rocks and stooped above him.

The boy was hurt—that much was obvious. As he dragged his wet limbs from the sea a jagged gash was revealed upon one thigh. It was bleeding profusely.

John leaned over the parapet and called: 'Hold on—I'll be down!' and ran to the steps hewn out of the rock below the terrace. Reaching the bottom he began to span the rocks ahead. Half way he met Susan and the French boy, who was holding his thigh in an endeavour to staunch the flow of blood.

'Let me have a look at it,' John said quickly, 'then we'll get you up to the terrace—'

'I assure you, M'sieu, it is nothing. A graze, no more!'

Anyone could see that it was considerably more than a graze. The gash was deep, but clean, and the salt water mercifully sterilized it.

'I thought I knew every inch of these rocks,' Pierre grinned ruefully, and John refrained from commenting that it would have been wiser to stick to the pool. An accident such as this could have happened to Susan and it was lucky that she had escaped. Lucky for him, too, since she was coming to work for him tomorrow.

The hotel produced a first-aid kit and John quickly dressed the wound, then, looking at Susan's wet figure, he said: 'The best thing now is for the pair of you to get dressed and join me for tea. I'll fetch this young man's clothes. I presume they're in a locker over there?' He nodded towards the Beach Club.

Pierre unzipped the pocket of his trunks and handed John a key. 'I am a nuisance, M'sieu, am I not?'

'Nothing of the sort,' John answered gruffly. 'And don't attempt to walk on that leg until I return. You can dress in the hotel and if you want a helping hand, sing out for me.'

When Susan rejoined them, a table had been set for three and Pierre was settled in a deck chair. John said 'Will you pour out, Susan?'

He decided that he liked Pierre Dupont and wondered just how much Susan shared that liking and whether the boy was important in her life. He didn't know why he wondered this, because, after all, it didn't matter as far as he was concerned. All that did matter was that she should work for him adequately. Her personal life was her own.

'It was a good thing it was your leg, and not a hand, that was injured, Pierre—if that's any comfort to you,' Susan commented.

Pierre agreed heartily and John asked: 'Why—apart from the general inconvenience of a bandaged hand?'

45

'Because it would be a greater inconvenience to Pierre than to most people. He relies on his hands for his work. He is a potter, you see. He has his own workshop at Vence.'

John was interested at once. He had paid a brief visit to the place which Picasso had made famous as an artistic centre and had been enchanted by some of the wood carvings and pottery made there. 'I've been promising myself a return visit for a long time,' he said, 'but the chance hasn't presented itself. Somehow work always interferes, but perhaps I shall have an opportunity in the near future—'

'You must make it!' Pierre cried. 'And when you do, visit my studio, M'sieu. I shall be delighted to welcome you and to show you round. I shall do more than that—I shall make a vase or a bowl or anything you wish, especially for you, as a sign of my gratitude for your attention this afternoon!'

He had forgotten his resentment of John's earlier interest in Susan; he even disregarded it now, for at close quarters the doctor proved to be older than he had imagined and Pierre believed that no girl as young as Susan could be attracted by one of this man's age. It was diffucult to guess what that exact age was, but Pierre was naïve enough to associate greying temples with advanced years. Then a thought struck him. Susan had said nothing about knowing the stranger who had watched from the terrace above, and at the time of their meeting he himself had been too troubled by pain to observe the fact that they obviously knew one another. Now the thought hit him forcibly.

'I did not realise, Suzanne, that you were acquainted with M'sieu le Docteur . . .'

Susan laughed.

'Of course I am! I start working for him tomorrow. Doctor Curtis has a clinic out at St. Maria—a clinic for sick children.'

'Which I, in turn, would be glad if you would visit, Pierre. You may be just the man I am looking for.'

'In what way, m'sieu?'

'As a potter.'

'I do not understand, m'sieu. Is it that your clinic needs some pottery? If so, I should be happy to make some, but hand-made pottery takes time, you understand. I say this to explain that if you require such things urgently, it would be better to purchase them from the shops.'

John smiled.

'No. I would appreciate your advice—and help, perhaps. I would like you to see my small patients and tell me whether you agree with my belief that pottery, as an occupational therapy, might be mastered by them. I don't mean anything so advanced as the use of a potter's wheel, but simple forms of modelling and moulding. That sort of thing.'

Pierre spread his hands in a typical gesture.

'Why not, m'sieu? Pottery is one of the oldest and finest of the crafts and its simple forms can be easily taught to children!'

'Oh, Pierre, would *you* teach them?'

The boy looked at Susan in surprise, wondering what prompted her enthusiasm. She was only going to work at the clinic part-time, wasn't she, just as she worked for other organisations in and around Monte Carlo? Besides, she hadn't even started there yet, so the clinic and its work, even the children, couldn't really mean anything to her . . .

Then his young and egotistical heart found the answer. She wanted him to work there because, in that way, they would see more of each other! Of course—it was as simple and as obvious as that! If he could arrange to visit the clinic at the same time as herself the arrangement would be an enjoyable one.

Satisfied with his conclusion, Pierre beamed.

'For you, Suzanne, I would do much, as you know, but first I must go into things, you understand? I must think the matter over. I must decide whether I can spare the time, for one thing. Do not forget, *chérie*, that I have my business to attend to.'

'I'm not forgetting, but I'm perfectly sure you could spare a few hours a week to making children happy!'

'As to that,' John intervened, 'the hours required might even be less than a few. Don't forget that these children are sick children. They cannot apply themselves to anything for very long. If you succeed in occupying any of them for as much as half-an-hour without tiring them, I'll regard you with profound admiration! When they are convalescing, of course, their stamina increases, but I can assure you that if you were generous enough to give of your time the demand would not be excessive. Nor would I be ungrateful. I had planned to hire a teacher, if one could be persuaded to attend.'

'M'sieu—I beg you!—do not speak of hire!' Pierre thumped his chest and grinned broadly. 'Me, I am healthy and strong! I have been healthy and strong all my life! For me, no sick childhood; no unhappiness! So what the good saints have been generous enough to bestow, I will make recompense for. See—I will come to your clinic and help the little ones! I will come once a week, to begin, and see how things go. Little by little, eh? That is how they will work and play and occupy themselves, and I will help them to do it. But remember, m'sieu—I am Pierre Dupont, the business man! Although I give voluntarily of my time, I cannot give voluntarily of my materials, so let us put this on a business footing right away. The clinic shall pay for clay and tools, such as they are, but only at the bare cost. My contribution will be the teaching. You regard that as fair—yes?'

'My dear boy, I regard it as more than fair! I regard it as generous.'

'Ah—me, I have the generous heart! Especially for the little ones. But more especially for my Suzanne. Thank her, m'sieu, not me. It was her idea, remember.'

John did remember. He remembered other things as he drove home. Doctor Pasteur had not arrived by the time they finished tea, so John returned to St. Maria without seeing him. Nevertheless, the visit had served him well in more ways than one. Briefly, he had forgotten Catherine's arrival and, even better, he had obtained the services of a skilled potter. And, as Pierre reminded him, he had Susan to thank for that. He wouldn't forget the fact any more than he would forget the glance of devotion which the boy had turned upon her at that moment, a glance which confirmed John's earlier impression that Pierre was in love with her.

Well, wasn't it to be expected? She was young—and attractive in her way. Like a wild flower, John thought unexpectedly, and was rather surprised at the simile for his was a medical mind, not a poetic one.

But when he had left them, and when he remembered their happiness together, he felt more solitary than before.

CHAPTER FIVE

The village of St. Maria stood high above L'escarène, and at its peak was the Villa Rosa—the house John had converted into a clinic. It was a rambling place, too big for private use, but ideal for his purpose. The series of bedrooms on the first and second floors had been knocked into long, airy wards, and the windows facing South enlarged to such a degree that practically the whole wall could be opened to the sky, thus obtaining the maximum amount of fresh air, so essential for his work.

In the distance the sea could be glimpsed like a vast blue carpet spread beyond the valley below. The view was magnificent and one of which John never tired. St. Maria commanded all the beauty of the Côte d'Azur, without its sophistication and crowding. He loved the simplicity of St. Maria, and the peace of it, and the perfume of a million flowers which everyone around cultivated to sell to the *perfumeries* in Grasse.

The fragrance met Susan as, with Catherine, she stepped off the autobus for her first day's work at the clinic. She stood for a moment sniffing appreciatively.

'St. Maria always enchants me,' she admitted. 'The fragrance and the peace and the utter simplicity of this village appealed to me the first time I saw it, and it has never palled. Sometimes, when my father was alive, we used to come here for picnics and sit on the hillside looking down on that wonderful view. Towards the end Father couldn't see it very well, but he didn't need to, he said. He knew what it was like and, once seen, it could never be forgotten.'

Catherine looked about her critically. She saw village houses, white walled and green-shuttered, with wrought-iron balconies and the eternal tubs of carnations tumbling their blossoms between the rails, but, like many French villages, the place was comparatively poor and so the plaster walls were peeling here and there, and paintwork chipping. These were the faults Catherine's sophisticated eyes saw and disliked; the picturesque quality of the village was lost upon her.

'A bit cut off from the world, isn't it?'

'I suppose so, but the villagers don't mind that. There's an autobus three times a day, which makes it a bit more civilised than some villages in the Alpes-Maritimes, but it is used mostly by sightseers. The village people are content to stay at home. And no wonder, surrounded by beauty such as this!'

'And the clinic? Where is that?'

Susan pointed to the white house at the top of the hill, standing square above the village like a presiding palace.

'Well, that looks well cared for, at any rate.'

It was indeed well cared for, thanks to John's diligence. He had painted most of the place himself, with the aid of one or two local workmen who were more than content with the modest wages he offered. The entire village was glad to see the Villa Rosa opened up and regarded it as a sign of prosperity that the establishment which had once been a symbol of wealth should be occupied again.

But it didn't flourish with ease. John lived for the clinic and the clinic alone. People only concerned him as far as their contribution to the effort went. He was a man of single-minded purpose and had found in this purpose not only an escape from disappointment, but complete mental satisfaction.

He took a pride in the house and grounds. An old man from the village tended the vines which grew up the white walls, and was gradually restoring to order the wilderness which had once been a garden. Men in these parts loved the earth and Gaston was no exception. Beneath his gnarled fingers, flowerbeds had been restored and a kitchen garden laid out, where food for the clinic was grown expertly and plentifully. Financially, this was a valuable saving as, apart from milk and flour and meat, food bills were kept to a minimum.

All this John showed to Catherine with some pride, and as he conducted her round

53

the garden Susan watched, with a sense of misgiving, from the office window. Catherine seemed to be viewing everything with great appreciation—a very different reaction from that which she had displayed upon arrival in the village. At that moment St. Maria had been nothing but an isolated mountain hamlet cut off from what Catherine herself regarded as civilisation, but if she still regarded it so she was careful not to reveal her reaction to Doctor Curtis.

The truth was that Catherine was feeling very much happier, for the Villa Rosa was all that could be desired—a spacious and lovely house in an ideal setting. The thought of living here, in close proximity with John, delighted her. The clinic at St. Maria was a complete contrast with the life she lead left behind—for good, she hoped. She wanted no reminder of those disappointing two years.

Susan turned her back upon the window and set to work. She was here as an employee, nothing else, and the relationship between Doctor Curtis and the woman who had come to work as his nurse was not really her concern. If it was an intimate one, as Catherine had hinted, Susan knew she would be wise not to see it; wiser still not to think about it. This man was a stranger. He meant nothing to herself.

The work was quite straightforward and for the next two hours Susan typed steadily from

John's notes—all written in his firm, characteristic handwriting. It was quiet in the little office, but she was conscious of a sense of activity about her, as if the heart of the place beat to a steady rhythm. Occasionally she heard the sound of children's voices from above and knew that they came from the wide balconies on which, as she approached the house, she had glimpsed a number of beds.

Gradually Susan became so absorbed in her work that she heard nothing but the steady beat of her typewriter and it was not until John thrust his head round the door that she realised more than two hours had passed—and that she had not thought of him, or of Catherine, during that time.

'There's some tea going,' he said, with a smile. 'I came to fetch you . . .'

She went with him to a room overlooking the kitchen garden, a room obviously intended to be the staff sitting-room when sufficient staff were employed to use it. At this moment only Catherine was there, already very much at home. On a low table before her was a tea tray over which she presided like a hostess. Her smile was welcoming.

'I'm revolutionising things around here,' she said. 'John tells me that his French staff never drink tea, so he has to make it for himself when wanted, poor dear! But now he's got me to look after him, all that will stop.'

She certainly seemed very efficient—and

determined.

Susan didn't linger over the tea. Nor did John. He went back to his laboratory as Susan returned to the office. On the way he said:

'I'd like to show you over the place sometime, if it would interest you.'

'It would interest me very much.'

'When you've finished work this afternoon, perhaps? Unless, of course, you have to get away.'

'Unfortunately, I must. Partly because the autobus leaves at six and there isn't a later one, and partly because I have to help serve dinner at seven. But I could come early one day.'

Catherine's voice said from behind: 'Do that, Susan, and I'll show you everything. Doctor Curtis is really too busy, and I know you wouldn't want to bother him.'

She was carrying the tea tray back to the kitchen and continued on her way serenely.

CHAPTER SIX

Catherine was right about Peter—he came almost immediately. She borrowed John's ancient car and drove to the airport to meet him.

Peter Collier was a tall, well-set-up young man, with pleasant features and an unhappy

56

mouth. There was no effusive reunion between himself and his wife, but she knew he was glad to be with her once more. His love for her was rather abject, and therefore irritating.

Catherine was resolved to stick to generalities during the drive to Monte Carlo, but he precipitated things by asking abruptly: 'Why did you appeal to John? I should have thought that he, of all people, would have been the last person to turn to.'

'But why? He's an old friend!'

There were times when Peter Collier was astonished by his wife. This was such a moment.

'John—*a friend*! Have you forgotten what he once was to you and what we did to him between us?'

'Of course I haven't, and this seems an excellent opportunity to repair the damage.'

'For him—or for ourselves?' he asked cynically.

'For all concerned!' she answered lightly. 'John needs you—and you need John—so what's the obvious answer?'

'That you wanted to see him again, perhaps.'

'Don't be ridiculous! All I want is to put the past behind us and start afresh. You in particular—and with the right man this time.'

'You once thought Stephen Foster the right man, even knowing him as you did!'

She rounded on him furiously.

'*Must* you rub that in? Anyway, you chose to join up with him . . .'

'Must *you* rub *that* in?' he retorted. Then he sighed. 'Catherine, can't we cut out this eternal bickering? I did hope, on the way over, that it wouldn't start again.'

'And who started it this time, pray?'

'I did, I suppose—I'm sorry, darling, but you must have known that I would never have agreed to your approaching John—especially on my behalf.'

'Of course I knew. I knew, also, that it was the right thing to do and a heaven-sent opportunity to get on our feet again, to cut out all associations we didn't want to continue, and to do a useful job of work. Oh, don't think I pleaded with him solely on your account! I was thinking of myself, too. Nursing at the clinic appealed to me strongly and when he suggested it, I jumped at the chance.'

'*He* suggested it?'

'Of course. Surely you realise I have some pride?'

She was never strictly truthful with him; never strictly truthful with anyone unless it suited her book. Peter was being tiresome about things—as, in her heart, she had expected—so the most effective way of dispelling his objections was to colour the picture a little more favourably. That, she considered, wasn't lying in the true sense but merely tact.

'Anyway,' she continued persuasively, 'you know you've always regretted the break with John, and you know you'd like to work with him again. Why else should you come? You could have refused had you wanted to.'

'With my wife cabling that she wouldn't come back to me unless I joined her?'

'Well—it worked,' she said brutally, 'and in your own interests, too. Do be sensible about this, Peter. We can't live in the past. We've got to think of the future and, more immediately, the present. Cut our losses and start again— and if we can start in a comfortable, ready-made billet, so much the better. You'll like the house at St. Maria. The village is a bit isolated, but maybe that's all to the good. At least Stephen won't be on our doorstep . . .'

'Since I've severed all association with him, that isn't likely to occur anyway. Goodness knows what the fellow will do now—medicine is the only thing he knows anything about, and he can't practise that . . .'

'It's his own fault. Don't expect me to be sympathetic with *him*.'

'I don't. I was merely trying to point out that he isn't likely to pester us when I can no longer be of use to him.'

'Nothing that man ever did would surprise me. You didn't let him have our new address, I hope?'

'Of course not. I didn't even see him before I left. There wasn't time, anyway, and we had nothing to say to each other. Not even about dividing what remains of the practice. The lawyers will see to that and I've left an inventory of everything that's ours.'

'Will it fetch much, d'you think?'

'A reasonable sum, I hope.'

'That's a good thing—we'll need something to tide us over until John takes you into full partnership.'

He looked at her in surprise.

'He said nothing of that in his letter.'

'He will—eventually. At the moment, the clinic is at the teething stage. It's up to you to help it to succeed—and to dig yourself in so thoroughly that when it does you're indispensable.'

He said stiffly: 'I'll pull my weight, but believe it or not, it'll be for John's sake. I know what this means to him—he dreamed it up in the old days. From now on it is work that matters, not money, to me. I've had enough of false values.'

They were driving through Villefranche at that moment. Ahead lay the beautiful sweep of its bay and the enchanted coastline which, thought Catherine appreciatively, must surely be one of the loveliest in the world. Oh, they were lucky—lucky indeed to be here! Peter should thank her for it, not criticise. She felt resentment stir within her like a restless whisper. I should never have married him— never, never, *never*! There's got to be a way

60

out, somehow. I'm sorry for him, but it's no use being sentimental about mistakes. I've helped him to get a fresh start, and he ought to be grateful for that, but I've got to think of myself. I can't spend the rest of my life with a man I don't love . . .

More especially when the man she did love was back in it again.

'Are we going straight to the clinic?' Peter asked.

'No—we move in tomorrow. John's lent me his car until then. My things—such as they are—are at the Villa d'Este. That's a small hotel in Monte, run by an English woman and her daughter. It's not a bad little place. I'm afraid you'll have to be content with a single room for tonight—there isn't a double available, so I'm keeping the one I've got.'

She hoped he couldn't sense her reluctance to sleep with him. Married life would start again at St. Maria, in the rooms John had delegated to them at the top of the house. 'You'll be absolutely self-contained and private up there,' he had told her, 'and that spare cooker from the kitchen can be installed in the little room off the landing. It has plenty of shelves and cupboards and should make quite an adequate kitchen. The only thing that top storey lacks is a bathroom, so you'll have to use one on the floor below . . .'

As if it mattered, she thought indifferently. She wasn't keen on the love-nest idea,

61

anyway—she and Peter had drifted too far apart to desire it, although if John weren't occupying the same house such an arrangement might hold the possibility of reuniting them. As it was, she would have preferred to share the general living rooms of the house with John, instead of being confined to brief contacts in the wards or during the course of work. That wouldn't give her much opportunity for getting close to him again— but at least, she reminded herself philosophically, it was better than nothing.

The trouble was that there was never an opportunity, during working hours, to discuss anything *but* work. Catherine had already discovered that. The small staff John employed—mostly inexperienced—required constant supervision. She could relieve him of a great deal of that, of course. She was a State Registered nurse and capable of acting as Sister. She knew how to make herself indispensable to him.

Peter said little for the rest of the journey. Catherine was glad of that. She wanted no more questions. Reaching Monte Carlo, she parked outside the Villa d'Este and took Peter within.

Introducing him to Ruth Lorrimer, she was unaware of Charlotte Fothergill's alert eyes observing them—and particularly Peter—with eager curiosity. The old lady sat sewing, as always, in her customary chair. Over

Catherine's shoulder Ruth observed her interest and was faintly amused by it, more especially when Charlotte's face lit up and, imperceptibly, she gave a triumphant little nod.

The meaning of that nod escaped Ruth, who was much too busy to pay attention anyway. She welcomed Doctor Collier and, after he had registered, handed the key of his room to Pierre. The old porter shuffled ahead to the stairs and once more the lounge was deserted, but for Charlotte and a retired Major snoozing in a distant corner.

Charlotte beckoned Ruth with an agitated forefinger.

'My dear—I've something to tell you about that man! I recognised him the moment he entered!'

'Charlotte dear, I'm much too busy to gossip—or even listen to it—just now!'

'You can't put me off like that, Ruth, believe me! I've an interesting item of news about your new guest and you ought to hear it. After all, if you don't know who you're harbouring in your bosom, it might be a rattlesnake.'

Ruth threw back her charming head and laughed.

'He doesn't look the least like a rattlesnake to me, Charlotte! In fact, he looks—and seems—an extremely nice young man.'

'Oh, well, if you *like* snakes—and some people do, I believe!—it's no use telling you

63

the truth about him, is it?'

'No use at all, my dear,' Ruth answered blandly, and continued with her work.

'Then I shall tell Susan! *She* ought to be interested—after all, she works at Doctor Curtis's clinic . . .'

Ruth looked up from her desk.

'She does, Charlotte—and likes it very much. From the sounds of things, John Curtis is doing a good job of work at St. Maria. He needs all the help he can get—'

'And this Doctor Collier has come to join him, I imagine.'

'He has. Why don't you do the same, Charlotte?'

For the first time in her life, Charlotte Fothergill was dumbfounded.

'I?'

'Yes. You need an occupation, my dear. You're too active mentally to enjoy sitting about, aimlessly watching the world go by. It's bad for you—*and* for your imagination.'

'So I'm imagining things now, am I?'

'I certainly hope so. Your inference about Doctor Collier wasn't very pleasant.'

'Perhaps his past isn't, either!'

Ruth glanced across the room at the sleeping Major. A loud snore confirmed her hope that he was sound asleep. She closed her ledger, crossed the room and sat down beside Charlotte.

'Listen to me, Charlotte. If you don't like

64

what I'm going to say, you can walk out of the Villa d'Este for good and I shan't try to stop you—I'm going to say it just the same. You're too nice a woman to spend your time digging up scandal about people. Why don't you do something worthwhile for a change?'

Charlotte gasped like a landed trout.

'How *dare* you, Ruth!'

'I dare, because I must. And I mean every word.'

To her surprise, Charlotte's indignation subsided like a pricked balloon. The corners of her mouth twitched wrily.

'And every word is true, bother you! I *am* a gossipy old woman, and I know it. *And* hate it. I never used to be like this, but there's absolutely nothing else in life for me now . . .'

'Oh yes, there is.' Ruth's capable hand touched the discarded needlework in Charlotte's lap. 'You can do this—at the clinic. Susan tells me they need someone to run the linen room. There's a housekeeper, of course, but she spends her time cooking and supervising the cleaning—she can't do everything. Meanwhile, mending accumulates and the nurses have to cope with it somehow. Susan brought a pile home the other day, but really it's a job that requires the attention of one capable person. Such as you.'

'My dear Ruth, are you suggesting that *I* should undertake the work of a servant?'

'No. I'm suggesting that you undertake,

voluntarily, the work of an expert needlewoman—which you are. You'd be doing a good and useful job, helping a worthwhile cause, and keeping yourself occupied in a commendable way. That would be something to be proud of and you'd find it interesting and satisfying, I'm sure.' Ruth looked the old lady straight in the eye and finished: 'Well, shall I ask Susan to tell Doctor Curtis that we've found the very person he needs?'

As she spoke, a light of interest touched Charlotte's face.

'Perhaps . . . I don't know yet . . . Here's Susan now.'

Everything Ruth said was right, of course, but Charlotte wasn't going to admit it—yet. She looked back at Susan's mother with a gleam of mischief in her eye.

'I agree that it should be interesting, my dear. Very interesting indeed. I'd be on the spot to observe this Doctor Collier more closely. *And* his beautiful wife, who came on ahead—without him.'

Susan's voice said clearly: 'And why should they need observing, Charlotte?'

As usual, she was prepared to indulge Charlotte's gossip, to listen to it and forget it, to make excuses for an old lady with time on her hands, but she was unprepared for what came next.

'Because, my dear Susan, that man Collier isn't all he seems. He isn't merely an amiable

66

young doctor who has come to assist another young doctor to do good works. He's a man who has quit Harley Street (which few good doctors do, let me tell you!) for the uncertainty of an experimental clinic in a country not his own. *And* he quit it in a hurry. And why? I'll tell you. *He's running away, my dear!'*

'And from what?' scoffed Susan.

'From a partnership which ended in scandal—*that's* what. And I shouldn't like to see Doctor Curtis's clinic ruined as a result of it! And it could be, because, as I told you before, mud sticks—even other people's mud!'

'If people choose to throw it!'

'Meaning that you think I will, my girl?'

'Talking about it could have the same effect—even if it's untrue.'

'But it isn't untrue. I have the cuttings upstairs. The story was in those papers which came the other day. I knew *just* what Doctor Collier would look like, because I'd already seen his photograph. I'll grant that he wasn't actually the guilty party, but like takes to like and birds of a feather flock together!'

'There's another proverb about empty vessels!' Susan retorted.

Her mother remonstrated swiftly: 'Susan—there's no need to be rude!'

'Oh yes, there is! Every need! John thinks a lot of Peter Collier—he told me so. And John wouldn't employ a doctor who wasn't decent and reliable! So I'm not going to stand here and listen to Charlotte running down someone she doesn't know, or spreading scandal which might ultimately hurt John! Whatever misfortune Doctor Collier has had, I'm sure it wasn't his fault, or John wouldn't have faith in him.'

Charlotte looked at her flushed and indignant young face; she looked at it for a long and searching moment. Then she said quietly: 'Good for you, m'girl! I'm on your side now, one hundred per cent! John Curtis must be worth helping if *you* stick up for him so loyally, so I'll do what your mother suggests— I'll help, too. You can tell your Doctor Curtis next time you see him that if the services of an old woman with time on her hands will be any use to him, I'll come to the clinic as often as needed and run the linen room, voluntarily.'

Astonishment and gratitude replaced Susan's indignation. She flung her arms round the old lady and hugged her.

'Now I know why we love you, even when you're exasperating! You've a heart, bless you, and it's in the right place!'

'Don't maul me, child, don't *maul* me! It takes half-an-hour to tidy this mane of mine, so don't mess it up with your exuberance!' Charlotte blinked furiously to control an unexpected rush of tears. It was years since anyone had shown her spontaneous affection.

Susan wagged an admonishing forefinger.

'If you come, Charlotte, it's to be work and

nothing else, understand? No gossiping; no chatter!'

'From the sound of things, I'm going to be too busy to have time for gossip, my dear! And maybe,' she finished with a wry smile, 'that will be a good thing . . .'

CHAPTER SEVEN

From the windows of his pottery at Vence, Pierre could see the winding road and, from the number of tourist coaches which travelled along it, estimate pretty fairly the number of visitors to be expected during the course of the day. Tourists were important, because they increased his revenue during the season—and carried away to their own countries samples of his wares.

He was an accomplished potter and loved his work. Like most of his fellow craftsmen he was content with his lot and not ambitious to make a fortune. If he were, he was apt to admit with a smile, he wouldn't be a potter, for in this ancient craft the reward was not wealth, but artistic and occupational satisfaction.

John Curtis lost no time in accepting Pierre's invitation to visit the pottery. He brought the subject up during Susan's third week at the clinic, suggesting that if she could spare the time to go with him, he'd be glad.

Susan went willingly. The pottery was a fascinating place and one she never tired of visiting, but in her heart she had to admit that this particular visit pleased her for another reason. Not merely because its outcome would ultimately benefit the clinic, but because she was to go with John.

Just why the prospect should fill her with such delight, she couldn't imagine. She hardly knew the doctor, as a person. So far their relationship had been purely that of employer and secretary—and why should it ever be anything else? The work was interesting and typing John's book absorbed her completely. If it were not for her obligations at home Susan knew she would have liked nothing better than to work at the clinic full-time, dropping her other part-time commitments. Not, of course, that Doctor Curtis wanted her full-time as yet, but if the clinic grew—as, indeed, it should— she more than hoped for the possibility.

Meanwhile, life seemed to have taken on a greater meaning, the reason for which she couldn't define. Travelling out to St. Maria on the autobus was far more inconvenient than popping round the corner from the Villa d'Este to the British Consulate, or to any of the other offices which employed her in Monte Carlo. But she had taken on this new work because it appealed to her—and, she admitted honestly, because John Curtis did, too.

Working for such a man gave Susan a

satisfaction which she failed to experience elsewhere. It gratified her to feel that she was helping a really worthwhile cause. Despite Catherine's determination, John had fulfilled his promise to show Susan all over the clinic and had given up the best part of an afternoon to it.

'If you see what's going on, you'll understand the aims of my research and find the book less tedious to type,' he explained.

This was true, but apart from that Susan was fascinated by the clinic and the work which went on there, and knew a desire to help more personally. She wanted to become part of the place. To belong. To contribute actively to the good it achieved.

In this, Catherine inevitably succeeded more than she, and Susan envied her ability as a nurse. It was the first time she had ever really envied another person and the reaction surprised her.

'I feel,' she admitted frankly to John, 'that my contribution is a meagre one. Typing is so impersonal and mechanical. I'd like to do something for the children.'

She announced this as they travelled to Vence in John's rather shabby old car—a second-hand vehicle which he had purchased on arrival in Provence. Climbing the winding Corniche he glanced at her in surprise.

'My dear girl, don't underrate your services! The aim of my book is to publish the results of my research and, ultimately, to help the whole medical field. In typing it you're making an important contribution to that aim. I've already won the interest of a well-known publisher, who guarantees a minimum printing of several thousand copies. The royalties will be divided between maintaining the clinic and contributing towards a very steady medical fund. So what are you doing, but helping the children—not only at the clinic, but elsewhere?'

'Put like that, it makes me feel better.'

'But why should you need to "feel better"?'

'Simply because the nursing side seems so much more useful than mine! It makes me feel almost inadequate.'

What she meant was that Catherine made her feel inadequate. She added without thinking: 'Mrs. Collier, for instance—she's a wonderful nurse.'

'She's a very experienced one and highly competent. I'm lucky to have her.'

As he spun towards picturesque Vence, John thought of Catherine with a rush of gratitude. She was indeed wonderful, working hard and tirelessly, and he wondered now why he had felt apprehensive about her coming. Not once had she put their relationship on anything but a professional footing; not by a glance or word had she reminded him of the past, so he thought of her now with tenderness and sympathy. He was glad she had come.

He spoke his thoughts aloud as he said:

'Yes—you're right, Susan. Catherine seems to have put new life into the nursing side. I haven't been able to afford such highly trained nurses as she, and the little French girls beneath her are learning a lot. In fact,' he finished with a smile, 'things seem to have entered into a new and fortunate phase since the day I met you. You must have brought me luck!'

'I'd like to think that were true—but in what way?'

'First—yourself. And then from the moment you agreed to work for me, things began to happen. Catherine arrived and, through her, Peter. Then, thanks to you I met Pierre Dupont who—again thanks to you—promises to be of further help. And we mustn't forget dear old Mrs. Fothergill! My housekeeper tells me the linen room was revolutionised instantly! Françoise likes her, which is fortunate.'

Susan laughed. 'It is, indeed. Charlotte is a dear, but she can get people's backs up. However, her heart's in the job, so all should be well. She enjoys it, I know. In fact, it has given her a new lease of life which she badly needed, poor dear. For years she's been alone, with nothing and no one to think of but herself.'

'Your mother's been good to her—she told me so.'

Susan said with simple pride: 'My mother

could never be anything else to anybody.'

That he could believe. He'd liked Ruth Lorrimer the moment he saw her—as, indeed, he had liked her daughter. As they pulled up at the entrance to the pottery John looked at Susan's ordinary little face and thought suddenly how nice it was. She wasn't glamorised, which was refreshing. She looked as if she brushed her hair a hundred strokes night and morning and washed wholesomely in soap and water—both practices which more sophisticated women would regard as naïve, no doubt, but the thought gave him an odd little sense of pleasure.

Pierre greeted them with a wide smile and wiped his clay-covered hands upon a piece of rag before extending one in greeting. He was delighted because Susan had also come and insisted upon opening a bottle of local wine to toast the occasion.

'To the little children!' he said, raising his glass. 'When do you wish me to start teaching them, m'sieu?'

'As soon as possible—it's up to you.'

'Wednesday is my best afternoon, when the kilns are loaded and firing starts. I commence no new work until the next day.'

'Good!' Susan exclaimed. 'Wednesday is my one free afternoon and I'd like to help, too. I've already tried my hand as a potter,' she explained with a smile to John.

He was touched by their enthusiasm, even

though he felt that Pierre's was largely due to the fact that he would see more of Susan, but this he forgot as Pierre showed him round the Pottery, taking him first from the throwing room to the glazing room, and on to the vast kiln shed.

John was fascinated by the place; by the colour and the skill and the atmosphere of achievement which only a craftsman really knows. A craftsman, or a humanitarian. The same sense of satisfaction came to himself when he looked at a child he had cured; the same sense of achievement was his when he realised that a line of research he had pursued was successful. It was the feeling of doing something worthwhile, for its own sake.

They lingered for a time, savouring the picturesque atmosphere of the Pottery, then Pierre insisted upon a visit to his living quarters above—a converted loft which was characteristic of his artistic, happy-go-lucky personality. He lived in a state of glorious confusion, for which he apologised only faintly, adding with a significant smile at Susan that all this would change when he became a sober married man. 'A home needs a woman's touch, do you not agree, m'sieu?'

John smiled his assent, but said nothing.

Pierre then opened a door which revealed extensions of the loft—wide and spacious enough to be converted into a comfortable apartment. 'It will make a good home, will it not?' he said with pride, obviously visualising things to come and seeking Susan's approval.

She gave the room a cursory glance and agreed with Pierre's statement without in any way committing herself. She was careful of that. Always, when Pierre hinted at the future, Susan erected a mental barrier behind which she retired, a little afraid. She liked the boy. They were good friends. There she wanted it to remain and she had never feared, until now, that it would fail to.

She was conscious of a faint embarrassment, and turned away. 'We must go,' she said. 'Doctor Curtis has work to do—and so have you, Pierre! I see a coach-load of trippers halting in the street.'

Pierre gave a mock groan. 'Alas, the tourists! How tiresome they can be, and yet how essential to my business!'

'You'll love them when they depart, armed with souvenirs!' Susan laughed.

'You are right! I must go and welcome them.'

'*And* charm them, Pierre!'

He shrugged elaborately, spreading his hands in a characteristic gesture. 'But, of course, *chérie*. As I said—it is my business, *non?*'

They left him at the door of his pottery, sending a greeting to the vanguard of American trippers who descended upon the place with the inexhaustible energy of people who had already 'done' the Confiserie du Loup, the Gorges du Loup, the perfumeries of Grasse—and were still eager for more.

'On Wednesday, then!' Pierre called after John, and they waved goodbye as they drove down the ancient street.

It was a brilliant afternoon, drowsy with heat, and for a while they travelled in silence. Then John said: 'Some tea would be a good idea, don't you think?' and turned unexpectedly into a wayside café.

It was one of those typical little French places, unimpressive of façade and unpretentious within, which unexpectedly opened on to an attractive terrace overlooking the gorge below. Beneath a vivid sun-umbrella John and Susan sat and talked, aware of a sense of ease which united them mentally. She had no difficulty in conversing with this man, despite the difference in their lives and interests.

After half-an-hour she wondered why she had been a little awed by him at their first meeting. When he dropped the mask of his reserve his personality was warm and friendly, and she felt as if she had known him for a long time.

Conversation lapsed into a companionable silence when tea came. They spoke desultorily, both willing to prolong the hour indefinitely. Then, to Susan's surprise John asked abruptly:

'Are you going to marry Pierre Dupont?'

She was so startled that for a moment she could only stare.

'I—I don't know. I haven't thought about it.'

'Obviously, he has.'

That was so true that she could make no answer.

'He's in love with you, Susan.'

The thought troubled her and she looked away, wondering why she should feel so embarrassed. When she bothered to think about Pierre she shied away from the possibility of complications. Why couldn't he be content with an indefinite friendship? Why must he spoil everything by trying to slide it on to another plane? Why must he get serious about her—so much so than even John Curtis observed it?

When she still remained silent, John said: 'I noticed it the first time I saw you together, on the rocks by Monte Carlo beach. You were sunbathing and your eyes were closed—but mine weren't. I saw the way he looked at you.' He hesitated, then asked: 'Are *you* in love with him, Susan?'

Instantly, she became defensive—because suddenly, and for no reason, she remembered Catherine, who had more than hinted at an important relationship between herself and this man. To her surprise she heard her own voice say: 'If I can restrain my curiosity, why can't you?'

It was the doctor's turn to stare.

'I don't understand—?'

She bit her full lower lip—a very attractive lower lip, a detached corner of his mind registered. A thousand questions in her mind demanded utterance, but she could voice none of them. How could she say: 'Is it true—about you and Catherine Collier? Does she mean something to you—something important in your life? Are you in love with each other? And why did she come here? Why should Charlotte Fothergill hint at something about which I don't want to know? Why should she imply that an association between you and this couple could be dangerous both to you and the clinic?'

It was impossible to utter any of these questions and for a moment something discordant and sharp flashed between herself and John Curtis. The moment was spoiled. Their companionship was shattered. Susan pushed her tea cup aside and said: 'Let's go, shall we?'

To her surprise, the man proved stubborn.

'Not until you answer my question. Are you in love with Pierre Dupont?'

'What right have you to ask?

'None at all—except that I want to know.'

'And if I don't want to answer?'

Because she had risen, he had risen, too. The flower-hung terrace was deserted, so there was no one to witness the sudden antagonism which leapt between them. He was angry, and couldn't think why. She was angry, too, but knew very well why—because her heart was thumping in an outrageous and uncontrollable fashion and if she stayed so near to him a moment longer he would surely detect it.

She turned on her heel, ran down the terrace steps and across the wild cottage garden to the lane where the car was parked. John flung a little pile of notes upon the table, and followed her. Susan took her place beside the driving seat, her clear young profile looking stubbornly ahead. She refused to meet his glance.

Before he switched on the ignition he said gruffly: 'I'm sorry if I was unduly curious. Naturally, I want to know.'

'I can't think why!'

'I should have thought it obvious. I don't want to engage a secretary who is suddenly going to leave me to get married!'

So *that's* all! she thought with a sharp sense of disappointment. *That* is all that matters to him!

The wild beating of her heart subsided and a provocative demon urged her to answer coldly: 'If that is your only concern, doctor, have no fear. When I do decide to marry I will give you due notice.'

She couldn't think why he should ram the gear so savagely and drive on without another word. Nor, if it came to that, could he—except that for some wholly illogical reason he wanted to take hold of the girl and shake her, hard.

And what that would lead to he didn't care to acknowledge—any more than he cared to acknowledge his desire to touch her. He couldn't think why a girl like Susan Lorrimer should be so disturbing, but decided that if she was going to have this effect upon him it would be wise to keep their association upon a strictly business footing henceforth. By the time they reached the front door of her home they were polite and impersonal again—an employer and secretary, nothing more. And a good thing, too, he thought angrily as he roared back to St. Maria.

Anyway, what did it matter to him if that boy and girl were in love?

CHAPTER EIGHT

After their stormy interchange John and Susan worked together in an atmosphere which was both distant and polite, studiously avoiding any personal discussions and confining conversation strictly to work. It was better so, of course—or so Susan tried to convince herself. But an invisible barrier seemed to have been erected between them and then she thought about it she was conscious of a bleakness in her heart.

It was in just such an atmosphere as this that they were working one afternoon—John dictating a new chapter and Susan studiously taking it down—when the office door burst open and Catherine stalked in.

She and Peter were now well established at the Villa Rosa. They had settled down well, Catherine immediately putting in longer duty hours than the autobus service from Monte Carlo had permitted before her husband's arrival, and Peter—after the first initial restraint—being caught up at once in the interest of John's work.

Things were going smoothly—more smoothly than the anger in Catherine's face, at this moment, would indicate. But at first John didn't see that anger, because from his window seat the entrance to the office was screened from view and for a moment Catherine stood there, door ajar, staring across the room at Susan in an excess of fury.

If John couldn't see Catherine, neither could she see him. Susan, she thought, was alone. And so she let fly.

'I suppose it was *you* who brought that garrulous old woman here?'

'What garrulous old woman?' Susan asked serenely, guessing immediately to whom Catherine referred. There was only one person to whom such a description could be truthfully applied.

Catherine slammed the door viciously.

'You know perfectly well who I mean, so don't pretend, Susan! That innocent little face of yours doesn't deceive *me*, even if it does other people. John may be duped by it, but not I! No one could have brought Charlotte Fothergill to the clinic but you, and I'd like to know for what purpose?'

'To work, of course. She's an expert needlewoman and we felt her talent should be put to good account.'

'We? And who may "we" be?'

'Mother and I, of course.'

'So now your mother is butting in, is she? I thought she had enough to keep her occupied at the Villa d'Este! I should advise her to confine her activities to it, if I were you.'

Susan's cheeks flamed. She, too, could be angry. She forgot John's presence completely as she retorted: 'Mother never "butts", as you put it! And don't you ever dare to speak about her in that tone again!'

'Catherine ignored the last remark.

'I'm still waiting to hear why the Fothergill woman is upstairs in the linen room and, moreover, why she has the audacity to order me out of it! John shall hear of this!'

'If you don't lower your voice, my dear, the whole house will hear of it,' John said quietly.

Catherine spun round; her face paled. He saw that her hands were trembling and felt suddenly sorry for her. After the collapse of Peter's practice in London she was, no doubt, pretty nerve-ridden. He could think of no other reason for her lack of self-control. In the old days she would have been incapable of such an exhibition, which proved how distraught she was now. In such circumstances, she should be forgiven.

So he said kindly enough: 'Mrs. Fothergill is here to take charge of the linen room for us, Catherine—voluntarily, what's more. It was an offer I couldn't afford to refuse, even had I wanted to, which I didn't. As Susan says, she's an expert needlewoman and she's doing a fine job of work. I appreciate it.'

'Of—of course.' Catherine pulled herself together with an effort. 'All the same, she had no right to order me out of the room!'

'And how did she come to do that?'

'I was checking supplies when she walked in and calmly announced that the linen room had now been put in order and if I wanted anything I'd better ask *her* for it!'

'If she rearranged things up there,' Susan put in, 'it would probably be easier, and quicker, to do as she suggests. It would save you time and trouble, I'm sure.'

'That's the answer, Catherine, so don't upset yourself.' John, tactfully, dismissed the subject—partly because it was wiser not try pursue it, and partly because two bright spots of colour burned in Susan's cheeks. Catherine's thoughtless remark about her mother had obviously gone deep. Somehow, that had to be put right and John wanted to do it himself, for two reasons. First, because Susan was becoming valuable to him and whatever happened he didn't want to lose her—and, second, because he couldn't bear the thought of her being hurt. Right at this moment it was the second reason which mattered most.

But of course, he reminded himself, he didn't want to lose Catherine, either. She was an excellent nurse and had revolutionised the nursing side for him. There had been room for improvement in that quarter and Catherine had certainly brought it about. Since her arrival he had been able to concentrate upon other things and now, with Peter to help him, organisation was speeding up. In time, he and Peter would be working together as harmoniously as of old. Already they had made headway, regaining much of their lost understanding in the unity of work.

So friction had to be avoided, and to ease the moment he said: 'I'm glad you dropped in, Catherine—you're just in time to see this—it came by the second post. Susan and I are feeling rather pleased about it.'

He handed over a letter which Catherine made an attempt to read. She was shaken by this unfortunate incident—especially by the fact that John had witnessed it. The realisation that he had been sitting there whilst she betrayed herself was galling. Characteristically, and unfairly, she blamed Susan for it, believing that the girl had kept quiet deliberately, that she had given no warning of John's presence because she was glad to let Catherine make an exhibition of herself before him. Typically, Catherine didn't take into consideration the fact that she had burst like a whirlwind into the room, flinging her wrath in the girl's face.

I'll get even with her! Catherine vowed. *If not soon, then later. I can bide my time . . .*

'You realise who the writer is, don't you?' John was saying, and Catherine had to force herself to read the letter again.

'*Dear Doctor Curtis,*' she read, '*The recent Press article about your work has encouraged me to contact you in the hope that you can help my little girl, Sally . . . She is only twelve and has been seriously ill for the past year . . .*'

There was more; details of the child's illness and a desperate plea for help, no matter what the cost. '*If you will agree to examine her, I will bring her to St. Maria immediately . . .*' It was signed: '*Diana Beaumont.*'

'You know who she is, don't you?' John repeated.

'Not the film actress?

'Yes.'

Professional interest rose to the surface of Catherine's mind, immediately calming her.

'But this is wonderful, John! Anything Diana Beaumont does makes news—we couldn't hope for a better advertisement for

86

the clinic! The newspapers will seize upon it!'

John smiled.

'The best advertisement would be to cure the child, which I'll certainly do my damnedest to achieve.'

'Don't underrate the publicity! We can do with it. Mark my words, once *this* gets around people will really begin to sit up and take notice . . .'

Suddenly she realised that John wasn't listening. He was looking at Susan in a way Catherine didn't like—a personal sort of way. There was also an expression in his eyes which she couldn't read—as if he were somehow concerned for the girl . . .

Fear stirred in the secret corners of Catherine's heart. Just how well could two people get to know each other over the cold formality of an office desk? Pretty well, apparently. Whilst she, Catherine, had been going about her nursing duties, grateful for a snatched moment with him, this girl was alone with John for long periods whilst he dictated to her. And in between dictation, what then? There were golden opportunities for conversation between them, for getting to know one another.

Catherine's jealousy was so intense that she said with some acidity: 'Well, *I*, at least, have work to do!' and with a significant glance at Susan she swept from the room.

When they were alone John said: 'Don't

hold that against Catherine—the exhibition of temper, I mean. She's just come through a rather tough time. I'm sure she didn't realise what she was saying.'

'About my mother, you mean?'

'Yes. It may seem unforgivable, but try to forget it, Susan. I'm quite sure she didn't mean it. Catherine isn't like that at all.'

Why did he plead for her so urgently? Susan wondered unhappily.

John's hand dropped upon her shoulder. She could feel the strength of it running through her like a current. Her reaction was swift and disturbing—a reaction of almost tremulous joy; a reaction so exquisite that she forgot her anger and her hurt, forgot even Catherine's animosity, in the sudden realisation that she had fallen in love with this man.

It was a startling truth, but one which could not be denied. It was also bitter and ironical, for she knew well enough that no one could possibly mean less to Doctor Curtis than she herself.

CHAPTER NINE

Catherine had a logical mind. Common sense told her that the best thing to do was to reject Susan Lorrimer as a potential rival. This, upon reflection, was easy. The girl was neither beautiful nor sophisticated; she was obviously inexperienced where men were concerned, and although she might he cherishing some naïve adoration for John (and that had become evident, at least, to Catherine) a man such as he was not likely to reciprocate, let alone notice it.

She had really nothing to fear from a slip of a girl who merely came three afternoons a week to wield a typewriter, and an extra afternoon, since Pierre Dupont's advent, to help with the pottery class. It was naturally essential that John should spend some time in the office with her and it was stupid to read any wrong interpretation into those sessions. He was writing a book, as Catherine very well knew because he had confided as much shortly after her own arrival. And, after all, men rarely saw their typists as anything more than machines . . .

As for the extra afternoon, the girl spent that with Pierre, not John, so its importance— or its opportunities—could be rejected.

Besides a logical mind, Catherine also possessed a resilient kind of optimism coupled with a quite ruthless determination. The combination of these qualities soon overcame doubt and fear, surfacing her again as swiftly as a diver. Once she had dismissed Susan Lorrimer she was able to discard the memory of that unfortunate incident in the office, and her heart promptly felt lighter. She at once began to prepare, with mounting interest, for the arrival of Diana Beaumont's child—the advent of whom would provide an excellent news story, no matter how much John, in his idealistic fashion, might underrate its value.

But he was unable to do that for long. Immediately he agreed to examine Diana Beaumont's little girl, things began to happen. The actress promptly cancelled a new film contract—and a fabulous one—in order to travel to St. Maria with her child, and the story hit the headlines. Such a story of mother-love appealed to the public and the newspapers did it full justice. They treated John's clinic in a like manner, splashing it across front pages and featuring the news that his old friend, Peter Collier, had joined him; his wife also, as a nurse.

Which brought about the very thing which Catherine didn't want; the very thing she dreaded.

Not that it happened until later. Quite a few days later. It was her off-duty afternoon and she planned to spend it shopping in Monte Carlo. It was a long time since she had bought any new clothes and the prospect pleased her. Peter had heard that the sale of his share of the Harley Street practice had gone through; his lawyers had even advanced a payment on account and for the first time for weeks Catherine's mind was at rest financially. She had money in her pocket to do what she liked with.

Throughout the morning her mind ran pleasurably upon her shopping expedition. The old black suit could be discarded at last; she would replace it with a linen one in pale green or deep blue—both colours which did credit to her colouring—and she'd buy some Italian shoes to go with it. The Riviera shops abounded in colourful Latin footwear and, with feet and ankles such as hers, she could wear them well.

And, of course, she needed some dresses. Sleeveless and elegant and up-to-the-minute. Sports clothes, too, and a bikini in some vivid colour to display to advantage the tan she was gradually acquiring. Her one-piece bathing suit seemed positively old-fashioned against such a sophisticated background as Monte Carlo beach.

She reflected with some satisfaction that she had the right figure to display a bikini, a costume which demanded perfection of form and line. She was tall, long-limbed and graceful, with not an ounce of surplus flesh upon her. Without any conceit she accepted the fact that she possessed above-the-average good looks and a figure many a woman might envy. It was her good fortune and she was accustomed to it and that was that.

The sudden access of money, coupled with the fact that things were going smoothly at the clinic and that Peter had settled down even more easily than she had dared to hope, lulled Catherine into a sense of security. She had been wise to take things into her own hands and to sever all connections with the past. In her heart, she'd been a little afraid that Stephen Foster might discover their whereabouts and endeavour to batten on them in some way. Whenever she thought of Stephen she felt a little flicker of fear . . . unnecessarily, of course, because the man belonged to the past and that was put behind them for ever.

So she discarded the memory of her husband's disreputable partner; discarded, too, the sense of guilt which troubled her whenever she recalled his name. But for her, Peter would never have joined up with the man—but why think of that? And why think of other things best forgotten? She had atoned for them by helping Peter to get a fresh start.

Besides, what was gone, was gone. And no one but she knew the truth, or was ever likely to—especially now that a new life had opened up, and a very promising one. She had nothing to fear. There was no risk that the past could catch up with her; no risk of any loose ends tripping her unawares. She had tidied everything off very neatly and with typical efficiency.

After lunch she changed from her starched uniform into the hated black suit. She knew it was elegant, well-cut and, like all expensive models, had years of life in it yet. She knew it would never date and that it became her well. All the same, she was tired of it and would part from it without compunction after today's shopping trip. So for the last time she took it from its hanger, brushed it and put it on, automatically examining it for any speck of dust and smoothing the skirt over her slim hips so that it fitted with never a wrinkle.

Scrupulous grooming was a thing in which Catherine took pride. She had never been known to appear with a hair out of place, or a crooked stocking seam, or a speck upon her clothes. Once Peter had observed, with a twisted little smile, that such perfection was difficult to live up to.

'If you'd relax a bit, darling, I wouldn't feel such a tramp in my old tweeds!'

'Then don't wear them,' she'd answered shortly. 'They make me ashamed, anyway.'

'*They* do—or *I* do?'

'Don't be silly, Peter! Tweeds should be immaculate always.'

'And uncomfortable? Can't a man be permitted to relax occasionally in a pair of old bags?'

'I deplore the very thought! A habit like that is a sign of laziness.'

'It's sometimes very pleasant to be lazy. Human, too.'

Really, she'd no patience with such talk and

said as much. Peter had regarded her with a sad little smile, and said nothing.

Why think of that now? Peter could be irritating, as well she knew, but she wasn't going to let him, or the thought of their incompatibility, spoil this afternoon's jaunt. In a little while—a very little while, she hoped—things would come to a head between herself and her husband, but she knew the moment was not yet ripe. She had to give John time to get used to their presence at the clinic; he had to accept her again without embarrassment. Once that initial step was overcome, he would inevitably be easier to handle; easier to influence. The barriers of his reserve would go down and all their old attraction for one another would flame up again. She was absolutely confident of that. The mere fact that it was necessary for him to be on his guard against her spoke for itself.

And when things came to a head? They'd all be very civilised about it, of course. After all, there were no children to complicate matters, so a clean and sensible break between herself and Peter shouldn't be difficult to arrange. Put, quite genuinely, she didn't want to hurt him. Even in her selfish heart a measure of conscience stirred. She wanted to atone, quite sincerely, for her inability to love him as he wished her to—and for other things, besides.

Well, she told herself briskly, helping him to get started with John again and to achieve some of his earlier ambitions should more than suffice in that direction, and when he was really on his feet, when he had thoroughly settled down at the clinic and regained a measure of his self-confidence, he ought to be able to accept the fact that a reorganisation of their life together was absolutely necessary.

After all, he knew that John had once loved her; that they had been engaged; that John had married no-one else, a fact which spoke for itself. So why shouldn't the three of them be sane and modern about the situation and handle it in a sane and modern manner? There was no reason at all why they shouldn't rearrange their private lives and allow their triple professional association to continue undisturbed. People were sensible about such things nowadays and Catherine resolved that Peter should be sensible too. She had never found him particularly difficult to handle.

So she was in a mood of superb complacency as she took one final glance in her dressing-table mirror and prepared to depart for her afternoon in Monte Carlo. She had plenty of time in which to catch the autobus, which stopped at the bottom of the hill not far from the gates of the clinic. As she smoothed immaculate white gloves over her long fingers she heard the sound of an engine approaching up the drive and, glancing out of the window, saw Pierre Dupont arriving on his motor scooter.

For a moment she studied him reflectively. He was a handsome boy and not, as she had already discovered, entirely unsusceptible, although it was obvious that his presence at the clinic was solely due to Susan. Nevertheless, he had the Frenchman's instinctive appreciation of feminine beauty and elegance, and Catherine found his obvious admiration for herself both satisfactory and pleasing.

She met him in the main hall. It was the first time he had seen her out of uniform and his frank young eyes ran over her immaculate suit with approval. She was chic at all times, was Madame Collier, and extremely attractive. He felt that Susan disliked her and couldn't really think why. The woman was charming and always had a welcoming smile for himself. Perhaps, he thought hopefully, this was the reason for Susan's dislike—that the basis was jealousy. The idea made him feel much better, for Susan had recently become a little remote, a little beyond his reach, their old *camaraderie* somewhat strained. The reason for this eluded Pierre and, therefore, annoyed him.

The chic Mrs. Collier flashed her welcoming smile very vividly at this moment and held out her hand to him. He stooped over it with continental courtesy, kissing the immaculate fingertips.

'So you're giving up another afternoon to the children, Pierre? It is good of you.'

'I enjoy it, madame.'

96

'So do the children, I can assure you. As for me, I deeply appreciate the help you are giving my small patients—the more so because it must make inroads into your own time.'

'Not at all, madame!'

'Catherine,' she corrected gently.

His white teeth flashed in a pleased smile.

'Not at all, Cathereen! This is the one afternoon of the week when my time is practically my own. Once the kilns are stacked for firing my assistants can manage without me for an hour or two.'

'It must be a most exciting place, Pierre.'

'The pottery? Picturesque, perhaps. You will visit it sometime, I hope.'

'I should love to!'

'You must get Suzanne to bring you, as she brought M'sieu le Docteur.'

Catherine's eyes narrowed, but her mouth still smiled.

'I will suggest it,' she answered carefully, and with a final smile—a smile which held a suggestion of intimacy and invitation which brought the swift blood to the boy's handsome young face—she went on her way, forgetting Pierre instantly.

So, she thought, Susan had taken John to Vence, had she? And when? *And* she'd kept the visit a secret, too—certainly neither of them had referred to it. Of course, common sense argued, there was really no reason why they should—but there was no reason to conceal it, either.

There was an angry note in Catherine's brisk step as she marched down the drive. What was John thinking of, to go careering round the countryside with his typist? If he'd wanted to visit Pierre Dupont's pottery he could have asked his Sister-in-charge to go with him, and arranged the visit to coincide with an off-duty afternoon. This seemed the most logical thing to do, since her opinion upon such occupational therapy would have been valuable.

The pleasurable anticipation with which Catherine had set out was now tinged with a sudden suspicion. Was the Lorrimer girl so guileless as she appeared? Sometimes these innocent little things could be deeper and more artful than one suspected.

Resolutely, Catherine discarded the thought. She could return to the clinic and its problems later; right now she was going off duty and was determined to enjoy herself. As for Susan Lorrimer, the girl was relatively unimportant and as for representing any sort of competition—why, the idea was ridiculous! She wasn't even well-dressed and could be dismissed accordingly.

A renewal of optimism asserted itself. By the time she returned from her shopping trip this afternoon, Catherine knew she would feel like a million dollars—and look it, too. The future was radiant.

So, too, was the sun. In fact, it was so dazzling that she had to shield her eyes against it and, in doing so, failed to observe a man lingering by the wrought iron gates; a man who studied the Villa Rosa with obvious interest. Not until he spoke to her, in his lazy, attractive voice, did she jerk to awareness with an icy sense of shock.

'Catherine, my dear, how lovely to see you! You're the very person I'm looking for!'

The man's head was silhouetted against the sun, but she recognised it at once. His face was in shadow, but she knew what it was like. She knew every feature, every plane and angle, every line of Stephen Foster's face, and she knew it with an intimacy she wanted to forget.

A sickening tide of shock ran through her. She felt her knees go suddenly weak and knew that the colour drained from her face. The man put out a hand to steady her, saying in concern: 'My dear, have I startled you so much? Forgive me! I didn't imagine for a moment that you would be anything but pleased to see an old friend!'

The voice was the same, too—deep and cultured and smooth. It held a menacing note which seemed to blot out the sun; a note which clamped down upon hope and made a mockery of her new-found confidence. She wanted to turn and run, but could not. For one thing, her legs refused to move and, for another, Stephen Foster's arm pinioned her firmly.

CHAPTER TEN

It wasn't true, of course. She was rid of this man once and for all, so he couldn't turn up here, in this isolated village, just as if they had parted only yesterday. And so sure of himself—as if nothing had happened to change their relationship, or to open her eyes to the truth about him!

She swayed a little in the bright sunlight and he said in concern: 'My sweet, you look pale! Don't tell me this mountain air doesn't agree with you? According to the newspaper reports, John chose St. Maria for its health-giving properties!'

Somehow, she gained control of herself and jerked free of his grasp. She even found her voice again.

'So that was how you traced us! Well—you've got to get away from here. At once.'

He looked pained.

'A poor sort of welcome, Catherine! I expected more warmth—from you.'

'Then you expect too much. And I won't ask what you are doing here, because I simply don't want to know.'

'That,' he said gently, 'is a little unwise, because it concerns you. Yes, you personally. No one else—as yet.'

'If you're trying to frighten me, Stephen,

you won't succeed.'

'Your anxiety to be rid of me reveals only too well how frightened you already are, Catherine. But why? I thought we were friends, you and I. *More* than friends . . .'

'Not now. I was a fool ever to be!'

'Recriminations, at this late date, are surely a waste of time?'

'They are indeed, just as this conversation is a waste of time. *You've got to go, Stephen!*' She cast an anxious glance to towards the house, a glance he didn't miss. She finished desperately: 'I can't think how you got here!'

'Very simply. By air.'

'I'm surprised you could afford the fare,' she commented brutally.

'I sold my car—that was worth a pretty penny, you will remember. You *should* remember, because we had some good times in it together. But, alas, the proceeds won't last any length of time on the Riviera. That is why I am here.'

Her face went rigid.

'If it is money you want, I haven't any.'

'Of course it is money! Surely you didn't imagine it was for love of you that I came?'

'You are incapable of loving anyone but yourself—with the possible exception of duchesses and débutantes . . .'

That was a mistake. She saw his cold eyes turn even colder, but he let the remark pass.

A footstep sounded upon the drive—a slow,

heavy step. Catherine drew swiftly into the shadow of an overhanging hedge, drawing Stephen with her. The footsteps belonged to neither Peter nor John, but, all the same, she wasn't taking any chances. A few minutes later she was thankful for the screen of foliage, for Charlotte Fothergill's elderly figure emerged through the gates and walked down the hill to the bus stop.

'It's only an old woman, Catherine—'

'But you don't know *that* old woman. She misses nothing . . .'

Catherine swore softly. She wanted to catch that autobus herself—she *had* to catch it, for there wasn't another into Monte Carlo this afternoon.

The old lady disappeared into the shade of the bus shelter and Catherine said urgently:

'Stephen—for the last time, you've got to *go* right away from here! You've got to realise that our association—Peter's, as well as mine—is severed for good. We can't help you—understand? You must help yourself.'

'Which is precisely what I am trying to do . . .'

He looked at her in a significant way—a horribly significant way—and she felt alarm twist in the pit of her stomach. That couldn't mean what she thought it meant. It couldn't! He had nothing on her—no proof, no evidence, no relic of her foolishness . . .

Or, dear God, had he?

She thrust the fear down and jerked: 'I don't

know what you mean.'

'Then I shall be only too happy to explain, my dear. Are you on your way to Monte Carlo? We will go together and over a drink I shall enlighten you.'

'I shan't have time for a drink.'

'If you are wise, you will make time, otherwise I shall have to call at the Villa Rosa to explain to you there—and somehow I don't imagine you want that very much.'

'Of course, I don't want it. Peter is rid of you, and I won't allow you to batten on to him again . . .'

'Your wifely concern becomes you, Catherine—a new guise, if I may say so. Since when have you felt so anxious on your husband's behalf?'

She was aware that colour dyed her cheeks—a guilty colour. In the distance she could hear the approaching bus. In another minute old Charlotte Fothergill would step out of the shelter and see them. Not that Stephen would mean a thing to her, of course, but to her inquisitive eyes any married woman talking to any man other than her husband was suspect . . .

Besides, she might talk. Next time she came to the clinic she might mention it. She might even describe the man! And there was no mistaking Stephen's looks. A tall, fair, good-looking man, with the profile of a film star. English, too. Very English. Oh, anyone who had seen Stephen even once would remember him!

The immediate problem was to stave him off and so Catherine said desperately: 'All right—I'll have a drink with you, Stephen, if you promise to let me go on that bus and not accompany me.'

'How else am I to get into Monte myself? I've sold my car—remember?'

'How did you get here?'

'My sweet, I came two days ago—right here, to St. Maria, on the last autobus of the day. You didn't realise I was so near, did you? I'm staying at the village *auberge.* I've been watching the clinic, with great interest, from there.'

'You *can't* stay in St. Maria! You must go elsewhere!'

'And where do you suggest? Think it over as you travel on that bus—alone—and I sit a few seats behind you, also alone.'

'I don't care *where* you go, so long as you leave this village!'

'That,' he said blandly, 'is entirely up to you.'

'Meet me for a coffee at the *patisserie* just past the Bureau de Tourism on the Boulevard des Moulins—the one beside the gardens. You can't miss it. I'll give you just five minutes—no more!'

He agreed, and let her go. He didn't get on to the bus until all passengers were aboard, so

Charlotte didn't associate him with Catherine. He was also the last to descend on reaching the Avenue de la Costa, by which time Charlotte had disappeared in the direction of the Villa d'Este, and Catherine towards the shops.

She was waiting for him when he reached the *patisserie*, some coffee before her and a cigarette in a hand which, he observed, was taut with apprehension. He was glad of that. The more she feared him, the stronger his power over her.

He strolled into the place negligently. He hadn't hurried because he knew she would be there. She wouldn't be so unwise as to break her promise, knowing that he would undoubtedly turn up at the clinic if she did. Her eyes surveyed him with a smouldering resentment which rather amused him. Catherine had taken the affair of the débutante badly because, of course, it was a slight upon herself.

What an extraordinary mixture she was! he thought as he strolled towards her table. Her anxiety for Peter, as they talked by the gates of the clinic, had actually been genuine—he was certain of that—and yet he was convinced she didn't really love her husband. After all, he knew her well. He'd been Resident Surgical Officer at John's first hospital at the time that Peter had been there—and Catherine, too. That was how they'd all met in the first place, and he had watched her pursuit of John with detached amusement. The girl had been mad about him in those days, and yet she had thrown him over for Peter in the end. She had possessed an overriding ambition, of course, and that ambition hadn't run along the same rails as John's.

From the beginning Stephen Foster had resented John Curtis, recognising in him a better talent for surgery than his own. That went for other branches of medicine, too. Also, the man was too serious for his taste; always studying; always working. Stephen, who enjoyed a gay life, despised him for it. All the same, as a partner in private practice John Curtis would have been an asset, and when that stupid business at the hospital occurred he had been confident that Catherine would succeed in persuading John to join forces with him and forget the whole affair. Instead, the man had refused, finishing his required time at the hospital and then coming here to pursue his dreams and ambitions.

'Well?' said Catherine, as he sat down opposite her. 'Come to the point, Stephen. What are you after?'

He matched frankness with frankness.

'If possible, a comfortable billet.'

'If you mean at the clinic, you haven't a chance. Anyway, what could you do?'

'Lab work, perhaps. Anything but medicine, of course. John might be persuaded to find a corner for yet another refugee.'

Anger flamed in her eyes.

'Peter and I,' she said quietly, 'are *not* refugees. We have no blots on our copybooks. You have. And you know perfectly well that John wouldn't employ you.'

'True, alas!' He spread his hands in a resigned gesture and finished: 'So—it will have to be money. I'm sorry, Catherine, but there it is.'

'And *I* am sorry, Stephen, but I haven't any. And if I had, I wouldn't give it to you.'

She gathered up her gloves and handbag, preparing too leave. She was half way out of her seat when something in his glance arrested her. She saw his hand reach for his wallet and open it. He took out a piece of paper and her blood ran cold.

'Not even for this?' he asked softly. 'No offers, my sweet? Then perhaps Peter might care to buy it . . .'

She sat down again abruptly.

'That's mine! Give it to me!'

'On the contrary, Catherine, it is mine. You wrote it to me—remember? You wrote others, too. Who was it said that a woman's greatest enemy was her pen? How many have incriminated themselves equally unwisely, I wonder? Shall I read this to you? It is very touching—passionate, too, I wonder if Peter would be amused . . . I doubt it.'

She no longer tried to hide her fear. It

shivered through her like an icy current. She asked numbly: 'Where are the others?'

'Don't think me unappreciative, Catherine, but I'm afraid I lost them—or perhaps, ungratefully, I destroyed them. Callous of me, wasn't it? But I didn't realise, at the time, that I might need them later on . . . However, even this little note might surprise and interest not only your husband, but John as well . . .'

'Let's leave John out of this.'

'I'm not sure that I'm prepared to. Scandal could undermine his clinical work. It could ruin his reputation.'

She laughed contemptuously.

'The fact that his nurse was fool enough to have an *affaire* with a man of your type is hardly likely to besmirch the clinic at St. Maria, and certainly not the man who runs it!'

'I agree. The only person who would take a serious view of that—and it *would* be pretty serious for you, my dear—is Peter. I'm quite sure John wouldn't approve, either. In fact, Peter might pack up and leave you—and who could blame him? And if he left, I doubt if John would want you around. I imagine he'd rather lose even a nurse than a good doctor— and Peter *is* a good doctor, after all.'

This was true and she knew it. Everything he said was true. If the truth came out she would win John's contempt, not his love. All the same, this man had something else up his sleeve. She was certain of that.

108

And she was right.

He said softly 'I wonder how many people have noticed the scar on John's wrist, and wondered how it came there . . .'

'If the truth about that were known, it wouldn't do *your* reputation much good!'

'The truth isn't likely to be known—only my version of it. If, for instance, the story got around that Doctor Curtis had to give up surgery owing to a wrist injured whilst operating under the influence of drink . . .'

'That would be slander, and you know it! It was due to *you* that John's wrist was scarred. *You* were the one unfit to operate! I can vouch for that, remember. I was on theatre duty at the time. John can vouch for it, too . . .'

'But, once the whisper had begun, once the doubt was there, people would be justified in wondering whether the worthy doctor was resorting to denial merely in self-defence— and his devoted nurse supporting him. Not much credence would be attributed to the word of a woman who would lie to, and cheat, her own husband . . .'

He saw her wince and continued blandly: 'Nothing is more powerful or more insidious than whispering tongues, Catherine. It would be wise to silence them before they begin . . .'

She took a deep breath and said: 'There's an ugly word for this, Stephen.'

'I know. In England, of course, it is a criminal offence, but what is the law in this country? Any idea?'

'I could find out.'

'Certainly, but you'd be most unwise to try because, in so doing, you'd attract attention to yourself. Even Peter might wonder why you wanted to know and it would be difficult to explain, don't you think? And difficult to hide the fact that when you began to be bored with your marriage you indulged in an *affaire* with his partner. So let's part amicably, Catherine. You do *me* a good turn by supplementing my diminishing funds with a small donation—shall we say fifty pounds?—and I will do *you* a good turn by giving you this compromising little note . . .'

'And how do I know you won't produce others, from time to time? How do I know you were telling the truth about them just now?'

'You don't. You'll just have to take my word for it.'

She lit a cigarette. Her hands trembled visibly and she didn't speak for a long moment. Then she said carefully:

'I'll strike a bargain with you, Stephen. If I agree to your "offer" you must promise to leave St. Maria immediately.'

'I'll have to collect my luggage first.'

'I'll see to that. I don't want you returning to the village—not even for an hour. I'll settle your bill at the *auberge* and tell them to pack your bags and put them on the last autobus out of the village today. It leaves at six o'clock.

110

You can meet it, and collect them.'

'And—this?' He flicked the note in his hand.

'I've thirty-thousand francs with me right now. You can take them or leave them.'

'That amount isn't equal to fifty pounds, but I'll take it,' he said. 'The bill at the inn won't be much, either, so I'm letting you off lightly, Catherine. Only because I'm fond of you, of course.'

As she counted out the money he said idly: 'By the way, who is the girl with the portable typewriter? I saw her go into the clinic yesterday and leave it a few hours later . . . the *auberge*, you will recall, is a convenient vantage point from which to view the Villa Rosa.'

Catherine answered indifferently: 'Only a typist John employs. There—give me the letter now, please.'

Her fingers closed over it with relief. She left him without another word. Her shopping expedition was off but, for the moment, she didn't care about that. Once Stephen's bags were on the autobus out of St. Maria she would feel safe. Thank God no one but she had seen him!

She didn't give another thought to his comment about Susan. The girl didn't enter into all this—nor was she important. But for a long time after Catherine had gone Stephen Foster sat there, thinking about John's typist. She had an intelligent little face; an interesting one. She might be well worth getting to know.

Such an acquaintance could serve to keep him in touch—or at any rate to learn how things progressed at the Villa Rosa.

He hadn't wasted much time during his brief residence at St. Maria. He'd spent most of the first day sitting at the window of his room, watching everyone who came and went at the clinic. Thus he had seen Susan arrive and, a few hours later, depart. He'd guessed she had something to do with the secretarial side and, on an impulse, had hurried from the inn and boarded her bus back to Monte Carlo. From there it had been easy to follow her to the Villa d'Este. Perhaps she worked there, too, but if she actually lived there it would be better still. So, of course, the next thing to do was to get a room there.

And the first person he saw, on entering the hotel, was Susan herself, seated behind the reception desk.

CHAPTER ELEVEN

A few days after Stephen Foster moved into the Villa d'Este, Susan worked late at the clinic. John had asked her to stay for the dictation of another chapter, but had been delayed by Diana Beaumont who, since her child had been accepted as a patient, visited the clinic at every possible opportunity,

112

lodging nearby in order to do so.

John encouraged her visits, knowing it did the child good to see her mother frequently. The only disadvantage was that Diana's anxiety made her thoughtless of others. It never occurred to her that to waylay the medical superintendent on every possible occasion might interfere with his work.

On this particular afternoon she delayed John even longer than usual, with the result that it was well after six before he finally got away from her and, by that time, Susan's last bus had departed.

'I'll run you home,' John promised. 'You'd better ring your mother and let her know.'

Charlotte Fothergill, overhearing Ruth's end of the conversation, raised a knowing eyebrow.

'I suppose you realise they're attracted to one another, those two?'

'John and Susan? No, I didn't realise it, but if it's true, I'm glad. John Curtis is a nice man.'

'What about Pierre?

'*What* about him?'

'I've been under the impression, for a long time, that he has a monopoly on Susan. You'd think so, too, if you saw them working together on Wednesday afternoons. That pottery class for the children is a great success, thanks to their efforts, but I doubt if Pierre would work at it so wholeheartedly if it weren't for the fact that Susan shares it with him.'

Ruth's brow puckered slightly at the thought of Pierre.

'He's a nice boy,' she said slowly, 'and I wouldn't like him to be hurt. All the same, I think perhaps he takes a little too much for granted.'

'Meaning that Susan isn't in love with him. My dear, that's obvious—to you and me, at any rate. But he's a possessive young man. He might cause trouble.'

'I hope not. Anyway, I don't see what trouble he can cause.'

'Jealously can cause all kinds of trouble, Ruth, and you know it.'

'Has he anything to be jealous about?' Ruth asked guardedly.

'Not yet, perhaps. But it's coming. You mark my words.'

Ruth frowned thoughtfully at her ledger, aware of a strange mixture of pleasure and apprehension. She had liked John Curtis from the very beginning and the thought of him as a possible husband for Susan was pleasing. He had reliability and integrity; he was a man, not a boy. The fact that he was English, and Pierre French, had very little to do with it; love was not a question of nationality. All the same, mutual characteristics of race and upbringing usually made for greater harmony and understanding.

Ruth pulled herself together. She was allowing Charlotte's imagination to influence her and that was dangerous. She herself had seen no signs of attraction between John Curtis and her daughter; certainly, Susan had revealed nothing more than a genuine admiration for the man's work.

She said thoughtfully: 'Doctor Curtis is a nice man, of course—'

'—but Susan hasn't said anything, so you believe I'm making all this up. Well, I'm not, my dear. Susan being the type of girl she is, would you expect her to shout secrets from the housetops? Maybe she doesn't realise the truth herself. I'm quite sure *he* doesn't. I see a lot that goes on at the clinic. I've got eyes in my head *and* I use them!'

'I'm quite sure you do,' Ruth laughed.

Charlotte changed the subject.

'I hear we've a new resident. A Mr. Ferguson, or something.'

'That's right.'

'What's he like? I haven't seen him yet. I almost resent the demands that linen-room makes upon my time—I miss the goings-on at this hotel!'

'As far as I know, there aren't any "goings-on",' Ruth answered mildly. 'Mr. Ferguson arrived a few days ago, ordered dinner in his room that evening and went to bed. Breakfast was taken in his room the next morning, after which he went out. That was when I saw him for the first time. The programme has been repeated daily, but I expect you'll see him

115

some time. He always seems to appear when Susan is around.' Ruth finished thoughtfully: 'And that reminds me—she was on duty when he registered. He couldn't produce his passport because he'd packed it at the bottom of a suitcase—tiresome of him!—and Susan reminded me to ask him for it. You know we are required by law to retain aliens' passports. I clean forgot it!'

'*That* sounds pleasantly suspicious—the missing passport, I mean. Perhaps his name isn't Ferguson at all!'

Ruth shook a despairing head at her old friend.

'I see that imagination of yours is still as fertile as ever!'

'*And* I hope it always will be! Life would be so dull without it . . . all the same, wouldn't you be surprised if I was actually right this time and the Ferguson man really was using an assumed name!'

'I certainly would,' Ruth answered drily, and continued with her work. But the figures in her ledger were suddenly meaningless. In their place she saw the names of Susan and John and was aware of a pleasurable hope in her heart. What if, in this instance at least, dear old Charlotte actually *was* right?

Had Ruth glimpsed the impersonal little office at the clinic at that moment, hope would have died, for there was certainly no indication in John's reserved face that he had any interest

116

outside his work. Looking at him from beneath her lashes, Susan saw the strong features and long, lean frame of the man and wondered how he would react if he knew she was in love with him . . .

He'd be embarrassed, of course. Nothing else. He'd probably get rid of her and employ someone more sensible; someone with a less responsive heart. So, at all costs, she had to hide the truth and that should be easy enough so long as she stuck to her work and spared no moments for dreaming dreams, or glancing up from her flying pencil to scan his attractive features.

They worked steadily until his housekeeper brought in a tray of coffee and sandwiches. The woman shook her head reprovingly. She was large, stout, and very French, with her black hair coiled on the top of her head and her bulky figure shrouded in the black dress which every respectable French housekeeper wore. John observed her glance of reproof, and laughed.

'Down tools, Susan, and take nourishment—or Françoise will scold me for starving you!'

The chicken sandwiches were good; so, too, was the coffee. John pulled forward an armchair for Susan and pushed her into it, gently. As his hands touched her shoulders she felt a warm tide of pleasure surge through her and averted her head swiftly. But not so swiftly that she failed to notice the sudden stillness in his face. She wondered what caused it. Not her own reaction, certainly, for she had been careful not to reveal that.

Since the day John had asked, so bluntly, whether she loved Pierre Dupont they had been polite and friendly towards each other, but nothing more. It was the cool, detached friendliness of employer and employee. He was amiable and considerate; she, pleasant and conscientious. But whereas she knew that he felt nothing more for her than an impersonal interest, she was only too unhappily aware of the deepening intensity of her feelings for him, and constantly on guard lest she betray herself.

She was on guard now, busying herself with the coffee cups and resolutely refusing to look at him. So she was quite unaware that for a long moment he studied her averted head.

Oddly, he felt that he was seeing it for the first time; seeing it as something more than the shining head of a young girl. He was bewildered by his desire to put out his hand and touch it—although it was not the first time he had experienced such an impulse.

He turned away abruptly and picked up her notes. 'You've got it all down?' he said at random and she looked up in surprise. He appeared to be studying her notebook intently.

'I thought you couldn't read shorthand!'

He grinned and threw the book aside.

'Nor can I—although I'm always fascinated by those hieroglyphics of yours.' He took the extended cup and drank the coffee gratefully. 'It's good of you to work late, Susan. You're a treasure. What I'd do without you, I don't know.'

'You won't have to do without me,' she said practically. 'Why should you?'

'Girls marry. Especially girls like you.'

Somehow she achieved a laugh, although her heart raced in the most ridiculous fashion.

'Marriage isn't on my programme yet. I'll give you fair warning when it is!'

She spoke lightly because, of course, that remark of his meant nothing at all. He was merely making idle conversation and she was careful to answer in similar vein. Nevertheless, their glances met and as they looked at one another the wild incredulity in her heart refused to allow her to hope. After all, he'd looked at her a thousand times, so why should she feel that this time he was regarding her in a different way? Wishful thinking, that's all it is, she told herself severely—and took another chicken sandwich.

She ate with the hearty appetite of a healthy young woman, and the doctor in him appreciated that. A companionable silence united them. She leaned back in her chair, her slim legs crossed, and was aware of contentment glowing like a lamp in her heart. This, she thought, was the sort of evening real happiness could bring—an evening in which a man and woman relaxed together, united by the satisfaction of work well done. There was no necessity to force conversation.

She wanted the moment to go on for ever. She wanted to remain here, with the glow of lamplight within the room and the late dusk slowly enfolding the garden outside. It seemed as if moments like this were suspended from heaven, shining and lovely as crystal, and as fragile; moments which could be shattered by one discordant note.

Unexpectedly, John asked: 'How old are you, Susan?'

'Twenty.'

Twelve years younger than himself; in some ways, she made him feel much more; in others, she was his contemporary. Work had made him something of a recluse, denying him the pleasures which other men took for granted; parties, dances, and flirtations had not been in his scheme of things and for the first time he looked at himself critically.

'I've never played much,' he said, half aloud. 'I suppose it's made me rather a dull sort of person . . .'

She answered in astonishment: 'It certainly has not!'

He smiled, thinking that she was really rather sweet. But perhaps that was too sugary a word for a girl so alive as Susan. She had plenty of spirit—and well he knew it. She had gaiety, too, and a sense of humour. He wondered if there was any other man in her life besides Pierre Dupont—in a place like Monte Carlo it seemed more than likely. He was still unable to discover what her actual feelings were for Pierre; whether he was important to her merely as a good friend, or whether she reciprocated his affection.

Suddenly John exclaimed: 'Good heavens, I forgot! There was a call for you earlier today, Susan—shortly before you arrived. I forgot to tell you!'

'Was it mother?' She couldn't think of anyone else likely to phone. 'I was working at the British Consulate this morning and came straight on from there . . .'

'No—it was a man, but, damn it, I've forgotten his name . . .'

The door clicked open and Catherine appeared. Peter was with her.

She looked very lovely in a housecoat of chartreuse green—a relic of the days when nothing less than a model could satisfy her.

'We came to put a stop to this late-night industry!' she announced gaily. 'You're to come upstairs, both of you, and have a drink with us—then Peter will run Susan home. I'm perfectly sure you're much too tired to do so, John.'

'On the contrary, I'd enjoy the run. As for the drink, you'd better join us for coffee instead or Françoise will never forgive us for leaving it!'

A brief cloud touched Catherine's face. She had managed to convince Peter, who had shown a reluctance to curtail a homely evening, that they really should persuade John to stop working, thus implanting in her husband's mind a sense of guilt because he himself was lazing whilst his partner was not, and after all that they came downstairs to find John lounging at ease with Susan and obviously enjoying himself. There had been an air of intimacy in the room, too; a contentment and companionship there was no mistaking. Well, at least, Catherine thought with satisfaction, I broke *that* up . . .

Peter smiled at Susan. 'I'm glad to see John's not working you to death, my dear!'

Her grey eyes twinkled.

'Françoise intervened and saved me just in time.'

Peter regarded her approvingly.

'I can't say she looks in the least fatigued—does she, Catherine?'

'Oh, Susan's always bursting with rude health!'

'What's rude about it?' John laughed.

He rang for two more cups, which Françoise frankly condemned. 'The coffee was for M'sieu le Docteur,' she said pointedly, 'and for Mademoiselle.'

'Then bring more,' John told her. 'No one makes such excellent coffee as you, Françoise . . .'

The woman softened, and departed.

'You certainly know how to handle that housekeper of yours, John. It's more than I can do. In fact, I think she resents my presence in the house.'

'Nonsense, Catherine. She went to a great deal of trouble to prepare the rooms for you.'

'Only because they were to accommodate Peter as well—which meant, she hoped, less work for her adored M'sieu le Docteur . . .' Catherine glanced at the litter of papers on his desk. 'Not that it seems to have stopped you from working at night. Is it really necessary, John?'

'Absolutely, if I hope to complete my book. Without Susan's help, I wouldn't be so far-advanced as I am.'

Susan, Susan, always Susan, thought Catherine resentfully. John seemed to be valuing the girl more and more as the weeks went by.

Catherine smiled at Susan particularly sweetly to hide her resentment, and to divert the conversation she enquired about the Beaumont child. That was a topic from which Susan would be excluded.

John said: 'We can cure her—I'm sure of that. Didn't Peter tell you?'

'I certainly did, Catherine. We were talking about it during dinner, don't you remember?'

She ignored her husband's remark.

'How long will the child be here, John?'

123

'Some weeks, at least. She may yield to my treatment quickly—I certainly hope she will. She has youth on her side, plus happiness. A happy child is always a more responsive patient, naturally. Diana Beaumont, despite her busy life, is a good mother. She's staying at Eze-sur-Mer, to be close at hand.'

'She can afford to—she's rich. You'll charge her well, of course.'

Susan detected a slight frown between John's level brows.

'Why should she be charged more than anyone else, Catherine? Sally's case is serious, but not extreme.'

'I've just told you, John—Diana Beaumont is *rich*! You want the clinic to succeed, don't you? Well, it won't do that without money.'

'Nor will it if I earn a reputation for swinging my fees according to parents' incomes. So little Sally Beaumont's case will be charged on its merits.'

'Did her mother enquire as to cost?'

'No. The subject wasn't referred to.'

'Which shows how little regard she has for money! Don't be a fool, John—cash in when you can!'

Peter glanced at his colleague. He knew that expression upon John's face—that unyielding, withdrawn expression. It was used as a mask whenever he felt anything strongly and wanted to hide it.

'What fee John charges is his affair,

Catherine, and I'm with him whatever he decides. I agree with him, too. This is a matter of ethics.'

John looked at Peter gratefully. Despite all that had passed between them, they still understood one another.

Catherine shrugged.

'Maybe I'm too practical—or maybe I merely have the interests of your clinic too close to my heart, John.'

His smile was instantaneous and warm.

'I know you have, Catherine, and I appreciate it.'

Suddenly and illogically, Susan was depressed. She remembered the words Catherine had said to her at their first meeting.

'We mean a lot to one another, Doctor Curtis and me . . . We always have, and we always will, . . .'

Later, when Peter had come to St. Maria, Susan had disregarded those words, but now they returned to taunt her. Peter, she realised suddenly, didn't mean as much to Catherine as John did.

As for John—just what *did* Catherine mean to him?

His voice cut into her thoughts abruptly. 'I have it! Ferguson—that was the man's name! The man who telephoned you earlier, Susan.'

She was surprised and wondered how the man had discovered that she worked here.

Surely her mother wouldn't tell him? They neither of them liked Ferguson very much.

'Who is this?' Catherine chaffed. 'An admirer? A rival to Pierre? Tell us about him, Susan.'

Susan laughed that aside.

'He's not important. Only a new guest at the hotel who is becoming a bit of a nuisance . . .'

'Pestering you?' smiled Peter.

'A little.'

'At least, he's got good taste.'

Catherine said lightly, just as Françoise entered with fresh coffee: 'What is he like? Tall, dark, and handsome?'

'Tall and handsome, I admit, but not dark. On the contrary—very fair. He arrived a few days ago.'

'He hasn't wasted much time,' said John, wondering why he already disliked the man so much. He'd even disliked his voice on the telephone, although the line was so bad that it was almost indistinguishable. Nevertheless, the smoothness had come through. The ingratiating smoothness.

Catherine asked, as she stirred her coffee: 'What did you say his name was?' She hoped her voice didn't sound as taut as it felt.

'Ferguson.'

Susan wished they'd change the subject. If John thought this man could mean anything to her, he was wrong.

Catherine's spoon echoed sharply as she

replaced it in the saucer, although no one seemed to notice it but herself. Her glance slid warily from one to the other. Peter was smiling at Susan, but John wasn't even looking at her. He wasn't looking at anyone. Just stirring his coffee thoughtfully.

Catherine drank hers gratefully. It was hot, piping hot, and eased the sudden constriction of her throat. I must pull myself together, she thought. There's no need for fear. Stephen's gone from St. Maria; by now, he's miles away. Just because Ferguson and Foster begin with the same letter, it doesn't follow that he's registered at the Villa d'Este under an assumed name. Why should he? And why should the long arm of coincidence propel him towards that obscure little hotel? It couldn't be so long as all that . . .

Besides, Stephen was much more likely to go somewhere ostentatious. He liked to make a splash, even if he couldn't afford it. So logic insisted that her alarm was unnecessary.

All the same, fear licked her heart with a threatening tongue.

CHAPTER TWELVE

John ignored Catherine's suggestion that Peter should take Susan home—a fact Catherine herself observed with displeasure.

127

As he drove through the night the winding Corniche unfolded before the headlights like a shining ribbon. The air was still and quiet and beautiful, broken only by the hum of the engine and the occasional cry of a night bird. Susan leaned back and closed her eyes.

'Tired?' he asked.

'Hm-mm. But nicely so!'

He gave a brief glance at her upturned face, etched like a cameo in the moonlight, and that disturbing emotion—that inexplicable emotion which had touched him earlier this evening—stirred him again. It was a long time since a woman had affected him like this. Not, in fact, since he had broken with Catherine, and even she had affected him in a different way. A tempestuous, exciting way, lacking the depth and quality of the feeling Susan aroused in him.

He was puzzled by it, the more so because he hadn't noticed Susan particularly when first they met. She had seemed nothing more than a nice, ordinary girl whom he was glad to have working for him.

When he pulled up outside the Villa d'Este she didn't invite him in. It was late and they were both tired. Life began early at the clinic and she knew he would be one of the first on the job.

'Goodnight, John—'

Unexpectedly he took her face between his hands and kissed it. It was a brief kiss, but

Susan was glad that the darkness concealed her swift rush of colour.

'That,' he said lightly, 'is not the advance of an amorous employer, but the kiss of a grateful man. You've worked valiantly tonight. I appreciate it, Susan.'

She reflected warily that she might have known it meant nothing more.

'Think nothing of it!' she answered inconsequently. 'It's interesting work. I enjoy it.'

He stepped down and opened the car door for her. His hand touched hers as he helped her to alight, and for a moment he retained it. Then he gave it a brief pressure and she turned and went into the hotel.

John took his seat at the wheel again and as he did so a man, approaching down the street, stepped quickly into the doorway, scanning the car closely, as it passed. John didn't observe him, a fact for which Stephen Foster was glad, for he had no wish to meet the doctor yet. When the car had gone, he stepped out from the shadows and, quickening his step, entered the Villa d'Este.

He was just in time to catch Susan as she mounted the stairs.

'Susan!'

She turned and looked down at him.

'I telephoned you earlier, today. I wanted you to dine with me.'

She really didn't take to the man called

Ferguson, and found it difficult to hide the fact.

'I heard that you rang. I hadn't arrived.'

He gave her the smile which he reserved particularly for women he wanted to charm.

'It seems that I would have been unlucky anyway. You already had a date, apparently. Who was the lucky man? I'd like to know the name of my rival!'

'He's no rival. I work for him. And tonight we worked overtime.'

'Then he's a slave-driver, but so long as he's no rival, I don't resent him.'

How like him to take it that way, twisting her words deliberately! She gave him a cool smile and continued upstairs. His step sounded behind her.

'Susan—why do you avoid me?'

She remembered her mother's injunction to be polite to all the hotel guests, so answered equably: 'I don't avoid you, Mr. Ferguson.'

'Simon, to you. And I think you do avoid me, Susan.'

'I'm a very busy person. When I'm not taking my typewriter to work in different offices, I'm helping mother here. It doesn't leave much time to chat with guests.'

He seemed to make absolutely no headway with her at all, but, unruffled, persisted: 'You still haven't told me his name—this man who is no rival . . .'

She was nearing her room. A few more

130

steps and she'd be rid of him. Surely she could be polite to him for that brief time? She smiled and said pleasantly: 'He is a doctor named Curtis. He has a clinic out at St. Maria. I do typing for him.'

Her voice was light and impersonal, but his shrewd eyes observed her expression when she spoke of John. There was pride in it. And something more.

The old familiar resentment stirred in him again. For days he had been trying to make some impression upon this girl—not, originally, because he was attracted by her, but because he could learn of affairs at the clinic through her—but now he was piqued by her indifference to him. Such a reaction, in any woman, was unusual in his experience. This sharpened his desire to create some emotional contact with her and because, so far, he had failed in this attempt, he blamed John Curtis—the man who made him feel inferior at the hospital; the man who refused, contemptuously, to join with him in Harley Street; the man who despised him. Stephen Foster didn't forget slights like that.

Susan had reached the door of her room. Her hand was upon the knob. She turned to say good night, but was silenced by the expression upon his face.

'Did you say Curtis, Susan—and a doctor, too? Not John Curtis, by any chance?'

'Why, yes! Have you heard of him? I'm not

surprised, if so. The Press have featured him a lot lately. The British Press, I mean. Some French papers took up the story as well.'

'I've been out of England for some time,' he lied. 'But I know the man's name. Who doesn't?'

'I don't know what you mean—?'

'Simply that it wouldn't be the first time John Curtis has achieved notoriety.'

'You're hinting at something,' she said slowly, 'and somehow I don't think it is very pleasant . . .'

'You're right. It isn't.'

'Then I've no wish to hear it.'

She was half-way through the door of her room. His hand fell on her arms, detaining her.

'I think you should, my dear. Your Doctor Curtis isn't all he seems. Look at his wrist some time. His right one.'

A chill ran through Susan. She had noticed that wrist often enough. A scar ran across it, sharp and thin, but she had never heeded it much. Once she had idly wondered how it came to be there, but hadn't attributed it to anything more than a normal kind of accident.

'What are you suggesting?' she asked quietly.

'I'm not "suggesting" anything, my dear. I just happen to know how that wrist came to be disfigured, that's all.'

'*How* do you know?'

'Anything that concerns the medical profession, or a member of it, always finds its way into the news. There's no profession on earth in which the layman takes such an interest—it has a unique kind of attraction. So, of course, when a member falls from grace—'

'What are you insinuating?' she said sharply.

'I'm not insinuating at all, my dear, I'm simply stating facts. When a doctor does something unwise, no matter how trivial, it is always magnified. But in John Curtis's case, of course, it really *was* serious. He attended a celebration lunch one day, and "celebrated" a little too well—unwise of him, when he was due in the operating theatre that afternoon. He "mishandled a scalpel"—shall we put it that way? And that, my dear Susan, was how he received that scar—and why he was dismissed. What price your worthy doctor now?'

'I don't believe a word of it!'

'Then forget it.'

'If you want me to to do that, why tell me?'

'I don't like the thought of a girl such as you being taken in by him, that's all.'

'Have you told this ugly story to anyone else?'

'Of course not. If the fellow's trying to get on his feet elsewhere—which is why he chose St. Maria, no doubt—far be it from me to queer his pitch!'

'You seemed intent upon doing that just

now.'

'I only want to put you wise to him because I should hate you to be hurt, Susan—not because I imagined you would pass the story on.'

'You may rely upon that, because I refuse to believe it!'

There was a sound farther down the corridor; the sound of a door opening. An old lady wearing a dressing-gown pattered along to the bathroom. Susan said swiftly: 'If you want to meet someone else who believes in Doctor Curtis, as I do, you should talk to Mrs. Fothergill! She works for him, too. Your story wouldn't go down well with her, believe me!'

'It's not *my* story, Susan—'

He broke off. The old lady was passing beneath a light and he recognised her at once. She had emerged from the clinic the day he met Catherine; she had travelled on the autobus with them. 'You don't know *that* old woman,' Catherine had said. 'She misses nothing!'

Which meant that she could be either useful, or a menace.

Susan said goodnight abruptly, and shut her door. He was left face to face with Charlotte Fothergill.

The woman glanced at him sharply. It was the first time they had met for, as Ruth had told her, the newcomer spent all his days in the Casino—one of those professional gamblers, no doubt. Charlotte despised them. A lazy way to make a living, she thought, and a stupid one.

Oh yes, he was handsome right enough. She took another glance and he smiled, bowed, and said goodnight. Her eyes sharpened. Somewhere, at some time, she had seen this man's face before.

She watched his tall figure as he retraced his steps. A turn of the corridor, and he was gone.

Charlotte hurried back to her room. From the shelf at the top of her wardrobe she took down a large cardboard box. It was filled with press cuttings, snippets of paper, newspaper sheets. Her nimble fingers searched through them and, at last, were still. She had found the one she sought.

CHAPTER THIRTEEN

Ruth was sorting the mail when Charlotte descended for breakfast next morning.

'Anything for me, Ruth?'

Ruth handed her a large envelope. Charlotte glanced at it and said eagerly: 'Ah— my knitting patterns! Those children at the clinic are going to need some warm clothes when the winter air descends on St. Maria! Sheltered as it is, it can be nippy in the Alpes-Maritimes in the winter. I thought I'd better make an early start.'

Ruth was touched by Charlotte's industry. The woman had found a new lease of life since helping at the clinic.

Ruth continued to place letters in their respective pigeon-holes. None, Charlotte observed, went in the one marked 'F'. She asked idly: 'And how much mail does our new guest receive?'

Ruth looked surprised.

'I thought you were too busy, these days, to be curious about your fellowmen!'

'I'm curious about this one.' Charlotte glanced around swiftly, then leaned forward and whispered dramatically, 'So would you be, if you suspected the truth about him!'

'Now, *Charlotte* . . .'

'For one thing, his name isn't Ferguson. On that I'll take my oath!'

'You suggested that once before. It's nonsense, my dear.'

'Have you proof of that? Has he produced his passport for identification?'

Ruth frowned. She'd been rather lax about that—or Ferguson had. He'd promised, several times, to produce it, and always forgotten. She hadn't pestered him. It was never wise to badger the guests.

'I thought not!' Charlotte exclaimed triumphantly.

To Ruth's surprise, she said no more. Susan was descending the stairs. She looked paler

136

than usual, as if she hadn't slept. She asked: 'Are you going to the clinic today, Charlotte?'

'This afternoon, my dear, when I've finished a latch of mending I brought home with me. Why?'

'I wonder if you'd ask John for the notes I took down last night. I'm on the reception desk this afternoon, but I'm not busy the whole time. If I had the notes, I could work on them here.'

'I'll bring them back with me,' Charlotte promised.

There was a sort of suppressed excitement about Charlotte today which even Susan, distracted as she was, couldn't miss.

'You seem very pleased about something,' she commented.

'She is!' Ruth interposed swiftly. 'A lovely batch of knitting patterns has arrived for her.'

Charlotte laughed and went on her way to breakfast.

'Mother—'

'Yes, Susan?'

'How long is Simon Ferguson staying?'

'I don't know, darling. Why?'

'No particular reason. I'll be glad when he goes, that's all.'

'Is he pestering you?'

'A little. It means nothing, but I don't enjoy it. By the way, why did you give him the telephone number of the clinic?'

'My dear, I did no such thing! Why should

I?'

'So that he could ring me there.'

'Has he done that? Well, he didn't get the number from me. He hasn't asked me for it. If it comes to that, I've never even told him you work there!'

Susan looked puzzled.

'Then I wonder how he found out . . .'

'Perhaps he asked Pierre—or even Charlotte.'

'I don't think he and Charlotte have met.'

Ruth was sure of that, too. Charlotte was an early riser and Simon Ferguson a late one. He breakfasted in bed and was rarely in for other meals. He went to the Casino as soon as it opened in the morning and, as far as she knew, spent his entire day there. Evenings, too. She didn't like him, but he gave no trouble as a guest and so long as he paid for his room she had no reason for wishing him gone.

'Mother—I think we ought to ask him to leave.'

'Good gracious—why?'

Susan was about to say: 'Because he could spread some scandalous story about John—a story I know isn't true!' But how did she know, except by instinct? The scar upon his wrist was there. The fact that no one knew him in St. Maria couldn't be denied. He had come as a stranger, to work in a country other than his own . . .

No, no, she *wouldn't* believe it! Her instinct

about him couldn't be wrong!

Her mother looked at her in concern.

'Susan, if this man Ferguson is annoying you that is quite an adequate reason for asking him to leave. Tell me, and I'll do so without hesitation.'

'He isn't—not really. Oh, he's asked me to go out with him, to dine with him, that sort of thing—but nothing I could really object to. I just don't trust him, that's all.'

'Well,' said her mother uncertainly, 'we'll wait a while and see how he continues to behave . . .'

* * *

Charlotte Fothergill was not a woman to let grass grow beneath her feet. The cutting which had featured Peter's photograph had also featured Stephen Foster's. There was no mistaking that handsome face, but without proof that the discredited doctor was indeed Simon Ferguson, she could do nothing.

And if she *had* proof, what could she do, apart from enlightening Ruth as to the dubious character of her guest? It would then be up to Ruth to intimate that his room was required—and so the man would walk out of their lives. That, as yet, Charlotte didn't want.

During the ride to St. Maria she pondered upon the situation. It seemed fairly obvious that the handsome stranger had followed his late colleague to this part of the world, but she doubted if Peter knew that. The more she saw of him, the more Charlotte liked Doctor Collier. He wasn't so fine or so clever as John, perhaps, but he was fundamentally decent— more so than his wife, she was convinced. Whenever Charlotte thought of Catherine she gave a mental sniff.

Even so, Catherine was a good nurse. She worked for the clinic wholeheartedly. It wouldn't do to let things be disturbed by the advent of Peter's shady partner, but Charlotte was perfectly certain that the man hadn't turned up in Monte Carlo just to spend his days in the Casino. Nor did it seem likely that he would remain nearby without letting *someone* at St. Maria know of his presence.

So, if Peter didn't know, how about Catherine? She'd be much more likely to conceal the truth than her husband. Peter hadn't the same emotional control as his wife. Charlotte had seen him betray his reactions far more frequently.

All this was guess work, the old lady reminded herself, and rejected it to ponder on just when and where she had seen the man called Ferguson. She was quite convinced that she had seen him in the flesh, as well as in newsprint.

The autobus jogged on its way. St. Maria came into view. Ahead she could see the village inn, and the rustic bus shelter opposite

140

the gates of the Villa Rosa . . .

And it was then that the shutter clicked in her memory and she saw again the tall, well-dressed figure of a man stepping on to the bus departing for Monte Carlo. She'd noticed him because he was the last to board the vehicle and in St. Maria no one stood aside to allow others to ascend first; certainly not the homely peasants who lived in the village. They were warmhearted and honest, but lacked social graces. It was always a free fight to get the best seats in the autobus, and tourists were as bad. But this man had stood aside, waiting to let everyone else on first . . .

His face had puzzled her then, Charlotte remembered, but she had dismissed it, convinced that she had never seen it before. She hadn't recalled the newspaper report. She'd been tired that day, and nodded in her corner. She hadn't even noticed that Catherine, also, was a passenger, until she wakened . . .

Catherine!

The shutter clicked again. Reason confirmed instinct and suddenly Charlotte knew, without a shadow of doubt, that her suspicions were correct. Catherine knew the tall, handsome stranger. She had known he was on the bus that day. But why had she ignored him? Why pretended not to know him? The answer was obvious. She didn't want to be associated with him; she didn't want to be seen with him, or to have her named linked with his. Which meant that he was important in an unpleasant, and even a dangerous, sort of way.

*   *   *

As Charlotte jogged towards St. Maria on the autobus, busy with her thoughts and speculations, the two doctors were sitting upon the terrace at the Villa Rosa, snatching a few minutes' conversation after lunch. Inevitably, it was work that they discussed—that, and the publicity given to the story of the film star's small daughter. It had attracted a lot of attention.

'There's one thing to be said for it, anyway,' Peter declared. 'The clinic seems likely to flourish as a result!'

'I'm already being forced to turn down patients,' John admitted, 'or at least asking them to wait until we have free beds. I don't like doing that. We'll have to extend. Open up more rooms. Take on more staff. We'll need a full-time secretary, too. I wonder if I could persuade Susan to take on the job . . .'

'She'd be invaluable, if she would.'

'It's largely a question of whether her mother could spare her, but I confess I'd rather have Susan than anyone else.'

Peter checked a smile. He thought he knew why John wanted Susan rather than anyone else, but wisely made no comment. He wondered when his friend was going to discover the truth for himself.

John's glance wandered over the terrace. It was weed-strewn and untidy, for Gaston had as yet had no time to get to work on it— cultivation of the kitchen garden had come first. On a wave of optimism John thought that before very long he'd be able to employ extra help for Gaston.

He gave a deep sigh of satisfaction. Things had gone well since Catherine and Peter had arrived and he was thankful, now, that he had yielded to her persuasion. It had all turned out so much better than he expected. Peter had settled down quickly and any restraint had soon vanished. In fact, it had been foolish to believe that Catherine's presence in the house could possibly be disturbing. On the contrary, she was gradually becoming indispensable to the clinic.

During the last few days John had even begun to wonder if he were working her too hard. She was showing definite signs of nervous strain, starting with that outburst at Susan the other day, and continuing with occasional flashes of temper on the wards. The other nurses, less experienced than herself, tried her patience, and he strongly suspected that they resented her arrival. In time the situation would sort itself out. In time they would accept her, of course. Meanwhile, he forgave her short temper and appreciated the valuable work she did.

She was wonderful with the children; untiring and devoted. This side of her surprised him, for Catherine had never struck him as being particularly maternal. Now he wondered why she and Peter didn't go ahead and raise a family. It would be the finest thing in the world for Catherine.

The realisation that he could think of Catherine as the mother of another man's children, without any shadow of pain, was surprising. A short while ago he would have shunned the thought. Now he could view it—and her—without any reaction but compassionate interest.

He hoped the change in Peter rewarded her; made her happy. Peter had become more reliant, more self-confident—in fact, stronger altogether—since coming to the Villa Rosa. Even the unhappiness about his mouth, which had been so evident when he arrived, had disappeared.

It was obvious that he still loved his wife very deeply. He watched her constantly; so much so that it sometimes seemed as if she grew restive beneath his scrutiny.

Peter yawned and stretched. 'Well, back to work!' he said.

They left the terrace, Peter for the wards and John to his laboratory.

'Is Susan coming today, John?'

'No—unfortunately.'

'Well, here is our devoted Charlotte, anyway. She's a loyal old soul, I must say.'

Charlotte carried a letter in her hand. She had met the postman on the drive and taken it from him. It was for Catherine, and bore a Monacan stamp.

Instinct made her conceal it from Peter. If it was an innocent letter, no doubt Catherine would show it to him. And if it were not? Then I'll have the satisfaction of seeing her face when she looks at the envelope! Charlotte thought gleefully. It it's from the person I think it's from—and the handwriting does match up with the hotel register—all my conclusions are correct . . .

Catherine was with little Sally Beaumont who, for the present, remained isolated. To Charlotte's surprise she was reading a story to the child and, from the look of things, enjoying herself. For a brief moment Charlotte stood within the doorway, looking at Peter's wife with a sudden flash of interest. No one was wholly bad, or wholly selfish, or wholly dishonest—of this Charlotte was convinced—but there were varying shades of character and Catherine's she had believed to be on the dark side. Apparently she had a lighter side as well . . .

Catherine was aware of the old lady's presence, but read the story to the end before looking up, unwilling to spoil the child's

145

interest in the tale. Then she closed the book and said: 'Time for your rest, Sally! Let me plump up your pillow—there! Comfy, now?'

There was a wariness in her glance when she finally looked at Charlotte, whom she frankly mistrusted. The old lady's eyes were too penetrating. Peter said she was really a dear old thing and perhaps he was right, but Catherine was on guard against her, just the same.

When the child was settled, Catherine turned to the door and Charlotte, who was standing there, held out her hand.

'I met the postman on the drive—this is for you, Nurse.'

For a fraction of a moment Catherine hesitated; for a fraction of a breath Charlotte thought she was afraid. Then she took the letter without glancing at it and thrust it into the pocket of her starched uniform.

'Thank you, Mrs. Fothergill.'

Charlotte watched her walk away. She was wily, that one! She'd never betray herself. But she was unhappy, too, poor thing. Unhappy—and afraid?

CHAPTER FOURTEEN

Catherine didn't take the letter from her pocket until she was quite alone. Out of the corner of her eye she had detected the Monacan stamp and fear leapt in her heart.

Ever since Susan's mysterious admirer had telephoned the clinic, giving his name as Ferguson, Catherine had sensed that her brief security was to end. Argue against it as she would, she knew that the new guest at the Villa d'Este was indeed Stephen Foster, and that he intended to lurk like a shadow in the background of her life, undermining any hope of peace or security.

So she wasn't surprised when she saw his handwriting; just frightened, and sick. For a long moment she stood with the letter in her hand, debating what to do.

If she had courage, she would burn it—as she had burned that incriminating little note she had bought from him. She would burn this letter unopened and leave him wondering why she didn't reply.

And what would he do then? She knew, well enough. There might be another letter, but he was much more likely to call in person . . . and tell Peter why he had come.

So she opened it—and thus confirmed her wildest fears. He *had* been lying, of course; lying in order to lull her into a false security.

'Catherine, my dear—I thought you'd like to know that I've come across them, after all—the other letters, I mean. Knowing how greatly you treasure your present marital happiness, I'm sure you'd like them to be returned to you—by the

147

same method as the first. I know our friendship will prompt you to help me as it prompts me to help you—and, also, I'm not so fortunate at the tables as I hoped! I'll be in the Salon Privée tomorrow afternoon (I can never resist the highest stakes!) and I shall look out for you . . .'

Tomorrow afternoon . . . that was today, of course. And she had to go. She knew she had to go. But what excuse could she give to leave her work? What possible plea could she think up?

On the way to John's laboratory she tried desperately to compose herself. It wasn't easy, but she had a few moments of grace upon entering, for to her surprise Charlotte Fothergill was there. The old lady was in the middle of a sentence when Catherine entered.

'. . . so if she could have them today, she could go to work on them. She's never very busy at the reception desk, and the hotel is full just now, so there'll be no more reservations to deal with. She could start typing the notes right away . . .'

'Don't you think she has enough to do, Charlotte? I don't want to work her too hard, or she might be too discouraged to come as my full-time secretary—as I hope she will.'

Charlotte said: 'Nonsense! Susan's young and healthy and it's obvious that she's becoming more and more interested in your work. The clinic means a lot to her. I shouldn't think she'd need any persuasion to come full-

148

time—and neither will her mother, to let her. Ruth's an energetic woman, perfectly capable of undertaking more work. And if she isn't, I daresay she'll be willing to engage extra help, if it enables her daughter to work for someone who means as much to her as you do.'

A glow of pleasure lit John's face. Catherine's heart stabbed. So it was true, then—true that Susan meant a lot to him. *But why?* Why that slip of a girl without any real claim to beauty or style? Good heavens, she was positively ordinary!

In the rush of jealousy Catherine's other anxiety suffered a brief eclipse. She looked at John's strong features and thought, for one moment of longing, how wonderful it would be to enlist his help; to lean on his strength; to be comforted, loved, and protected by him. If she confided the truth to him, *he* would know how to deal with Stephen Foster; he'd send the man packing, and that would be that. He had always been the stronger of the two; the only man Stephen could not stand up against . . .

For a moment, Catherine weakened, but only for a moment. Then common sense returned. To confide in John would mean confiding everything—the compromising letters Stephen had in his possession, and how he had come by them, and when, and why . . . she would have to reveal herself for the person she was, the person she was beginning to despise. And he would despise her, too.

John's good opinion was the only thing she had left and she meant to fight for it. Sometimes she felt that Peter didn't think as much of her as John did; sometimes, of late, her husband looked at her as if he were seeing right through her. She even felt that he was waiting for her to speak, to confess, to own up . . . As if it wasn't bad enough to be tortured by Stephen, without having Peter suspicious and watchful!

But what had made him so? Her manner? It was true that she was always on the defensive with him, afraid of betraying herself, afraid of letting him see that she still loved John, but surely he didn't suspect the truth? Surely he didn't guess, when she yielded to his love, that she did so only from a sense of duty, plus a desire to hide her heart?

She became aware that she must have been standing there, just inside the laboratory door, for a few moments, because John was looking at her in an enquiring way. Charlotte, too, was watching her.

'What is it, Catherine? Aren't you well? You look pale . . .'

His voice was full of kindly concern and, ridiculously, she wanted to cry. It was a long time since she had cried, and now the desire was prompted by the kindness in his voice—a kindness which was nothing but brotherly. For Susan, of course, it would have been different—tender and personal; the feeling of a man for a woman . . .

Anger came to Catherine's rescue; anger and jealousy and a renewal of determination. She wasn't going to let a slip of a girl come between herself and John! What else had she been fighting for since coming to St. Maria, but to get him back? And when she succeeded, she would go to Peter and be honest with him at last.

'I've a raging toothache!' she said at random. 'I came to see if I could go into Monte Carlo to find a dentist . . .'

'There's a good one just round the corner from the Villa d'Este,' Charlotte told her. 'Jean Duval. Mrs. Lorrimer recommends him to hotel guests, so he should be good.' The old lady chuckled. 'I can't speak first-hand, not having any teeth of my own to ache!'

Catherine smiled weakly, and thanked her.

John was sympathetic and concerned: 'I'd run you there, Catherine, but unfortunately I'm tied up for the afternoon. So is Peter, I know. But you can't go by bus—do you feel fit enough to drive? If so, take my car.'

This was one occasion when she was thankful John couldn't accompany her. She had to visit the Casino and find Stephen in the Salon Privée and no one—absolutely *no one*—must know!

So she took the car and as she drove it round from the garage she remembered Charlotte's remark about Susan's work—

something about getting on with it this afternoon, if she had the notes to work from. Catherine's alert brain moved quickly. A few minutes with Susan could be put to good account . . .

When she finally drove down the Grande Corniche the notes for Susan were in her bag and, in her heart, determination vied with her despair.

*   *   *

Susan, as she expected, sat behind the reception desk, alone. Catherine was glad Mrs. Lorrimer was not around.

'I brought these,' she said amiably. 'I understand you want to go ahead with the typing . . .'

'I do, indeed. Thank you, Catherine.'

There seemed nothing more to say, but Catherine lingered.

'Will you manage to complete them?' she asked conversationally.

'Not this afternoon, of course, but I'll make a good start.'

'I didn't mean this afternoon—I mean before the new secretary takes over.'

Susan stared.

'What new secretary?'

'Oh, dear—hasn't John said anything? Naturally, I thought you knew. Perhaps it would be wise not to tell him I mentioned it, because I expect he'll want to break the news himself. But I heard him discussing it only today and you'll have to know some time . . . The clinic is expanding rapidly, so he has decided to engage a full-time secretary. I expect you'll be glad not to go trailing up to St. Maria on that ghastly little autobus, won't you?'

'No—' jerked Susan. 'I'll be sorry.'

'Darling, so will we all be—sorry to lose you, I mean—but you do see John's point, don't you?' Catherine's voice adopted a note of sage advice: 'If I were you, Susan, I'd look around for something else at once and let him know when next you go to the clinic. You can easily get more work, can't you?'

'Very easily indeed! In fact, only yesterday the Consulate asked me to put in longer hours. I'll let them know, at once, that I'm free to.'

'Darling, I'm so glad—for you, I mean. The Consulate is almost on your doorstep, isn't it? John will be pleased, too, I'm certain of that. He won't feel so badly about dismissing you . . .'

CHAPTER FIFTEEN

The day after Susan learned of John's decision to dismiss her, she was due to help Pierre's pottery class. She hoped she wouldn't meet John; she wasn't ready to face him yet,

153

although she had taken Catherine's advice and promptly acted upon it. The British Consulate had been pleased to hear that she would soon be free to undertake more typing for them.

The matter was settled at once. When she replaced the telephone receiver Susan felt as if she had thrown away part of her heart.

To stifle thought, she worked diligently the whole afternoon. Charlotte returned from St. Maria about six and only interrupted her to say: 'Where's your mother, dear? I want to talk to her.'

'She'll be in the kitchen, I expect, supervising dinner. I shouldn't bother her now, Charlotte.'

'All right, my dear. I'll wait until later.'

Susan hadn't stopped typing, and Charlotte shuffled on her way. A few minutes later Simon Ferguson came through the front door, evidently in high spirits. Pausing beside her desk he remarked: 'I don't like to see a young girl in bondage. Why don't you put your cover on that typewriter, and step out with me tonight? What about a flutter at the Casino?'

'I'm sorry—I don't gamble. I can't afford it.'

'But I can, my dear! Funds have just arrived from England.'

'How nice for you.'

'Nice for both of us, if you'll only relax and have fun. Don't misunderstand me, Susan—I *mean* fun. Come to the Sporting Club with me tomorrow evening—they're holding a gala dance to celebrate the Monte Carlo Rally. Don your best bib and tucker and let's enjoy ourselves!'

He was nicer in that mood—gay and rather charming. The invitation was friendly, nothing more, and it certainly presented a further escape from thought. Susan felt in the moodl to do something reckless, like throwing her cap over the nearest windmill and chancing who caught it the other side. It certainly wouldn't be John, she thought miserably.

So she cried: 'I'd love to go!' and the matter was settled there and then.

But as she wedged clay for the children the following afternoon Susan knew she regretted accepting the invitation. Would it really help, to go dancing with a man like Simon Ferguson? Would it really take her mind off John, and the pain she felt at the thought that he intended to dismiss her?

The door burst open and Pierre entered with a flourish, kissing her soundly on both cheeks. She had a feeling that Pierre only came to the clinic in order to see her, fond as he was of the children and patient as he was with their efforts. The thought disappointed her. He had been lavish in his gratitude to John that day on the beach, but had he really meant it when saying that he would organise this class as a sign of his appreciation?

Susan decided not to tell him she was leaving. He would know soon enough. If she told him in advance he might decide to follow suit, and she had no wish for that to happen. She had become interested in the pottery class and was anxious for it to continue, but if Pierre knew the truth he might, on a wave of indignation, refuse to come any more. He was impetuous and passionate, as well she knew. He was also young—lately, he seemed to her younger than she had realised—and not a little spoilt. Pierre was handsome and much appreciated by the local French girls.

The class was restive that afternoon. John had prepared Pierre for such an eventuality, warning him at the beginning that convalescent children lacked the normal concentration of those who were healthy. Today one small boy found it more entertaining to make pellets of the clay and fling them at his companions, and when one finally landed a bull's eye Susan suggested it was time to pack up.

Pierre cast an eloquent glance towards heaven and agreed. He was fond of the little demons, but thankful, more often than not, to say goodbye to them.

'I wonder why I ever imagined this half-hour would be a relaxation, *chérie?* My workshop is infinitely more peaceful!'

She smiled, wondering how he would cope with the class single-handed.

As they supervised the clearing up, Catherine entered. Susan had to admit that in caring for her small patients Catherine was diligent. She frequently dropped in to make sure that no child was tiring and had insisted that Pierre should let her know the minute he felt the children had had enough for one day. Now she smiled at him and commented sympathetically: 'Finishing early, Pierre? Have the children been playing you up?'

'Not exactly, Madame—just a little more energetic than usual, that is all. Who said *les enfants* were ill?'

She laughed, marshalling the little ones before carrying them off for tea.

'You do wonders with them, all the same, Pierre.'

'Not I,' he admitted frankly. 'I should be quite inadequate alone. It is thanks to Susan that I survive!'

Catherine said nothing; nor did she glance in Susan's direction. Susan was glad of that, although she knew she had cause to be grateful to Catherine who had, after all, saved her pride. Thanks to the nurse's timely warning she would be able to tender her notice before John could humiliate her with dismissal.

Even though logic argued that John's decision to engage a full-time secretary was a natural one, in view of the increasing growth of the clinic, and therefore cast no reflection upon her own capabilities, Susan was hurt. Even though reason argued that he was justified in assuming that her other commitments would leave her no time to put in extra hours, she still felt that in discussing her dismissal with others he had behaved badly. So she was glad she had heeded Catherine's advice—and grateful for the warning.

She picked up the smallest child whilst Pierre took the hands of two others and followed Catherine's uniformed figure back to the wards. Walking along the corridor, Pierre said: 'I suppose, Suzanne, you will be staying for that English ritual this afternoon? If so, I will wait—if,' he added with an accustomed hesitation, 'you will permit me?'

Susan laughed.

'I presume you mean tea, Pierre? No—I won't be staying. Not today.'

He looked pleased.

'Then I will take you back to Monte Carlo on my Lambretta!'

She was grateful for the offer. Leaving early, she avoided John, who worked in his laboratory until tea-time each day. She knew it was cowardly to avoid the moment. She would have to face up to it tomorrow. But by that tune, she reflected, she should have got over the initial hurt and be well prepared to hand in her resignation without self-consciousness or embarrassment.

Pierre spun recklessly down the precipitous Corniche and was surprised when Susan uttered no protest. Indeed, she seemed hardly aware that he skidded round hairpin bends and zoomed downhill without braking. In view of the fact that he was deliberately trying to rouse her from a detached sort of silence which he could neither understand nor account for, her reaction—or lack of it-perturbed him. Lately, Susan seemed to be eluding him. Their companionable ease with one another was becoming strained, and he couldn't think why. It was as if she had moved to another plane of thought, and left him behind.

So he was in no good humour when they reached the Villa d'Este and met Simon Ferguson face to face. The man was coming out of the hotel and his blonde head shone smoothly and handsomely. Pierre disliked him, although he had only met him once before. He disliked the arrogant self-confidence, the immaculate tailoring—which a struggling potter could hardly afford—and the general air of decadent charm about the man; but more than all he disliked the way in which he regarded Susan.

And particularly at this moment. Normally, it might be possible to overlook a roving eye and unconcealed admiration, but today there was an additional quality—a possessive quality. He smiled a welcome which was almost familiar, lifted a graceful hand in greeting, and said lazily: 'Ah, Susan, my sweet!

Don't forget tonight. I'll be ready and waiting at eight o'clock sharp . . .'

Pierre propped his motor scooter beside the pavement and followed Susan into the hotel.

'And who, may I ask, was that, *chérie*?'

The lounge was empty, for which Susan was glad. Pierre was evidently building up for a scene and when in such a mood not even the whole world could stop him.

She answered soothingly: 'You know perfectly well, Pierre. I introduced you shortly after he arrived. His name is Ferguson. Simon Ferguson.'

'I dislike him!'

'So do I, somehow.'

'*Nom du nom*—then why go out with him?' Pointing a furious finger at her he commanded: 'Do not deny it, Suzanne—you are spending this evening with that man!'

'I wasn't going to deny it.'

'Why? Why? *Why* you go with him?'

Susan ran a hand wearily through her hair.

'Really, Pierre, you've no right to question me like this!' She felt resentment chafing her mind like sand against the skin.

'No right! *I*—who am going to marry you! You say I have no *right*!'

Susan's hand dropped limply from her hair; her mouth fell open.

'Pierre—I have never promised to marry you!'

'Because there is no need!' He was excited

160

and voluble and exceedingly French all at once. 'Always it has been understood!'

'By you, perhaps. But not by me.'

'Suzanne!' He seized her shoulders and said firmly: 'Listen to me, *chérie*—I will not allow you to go out with any other man but me. I will not allow you to *marry* any man but me!'

She jerked away. Now she was angry—too angry to feel sorry for him.

'And *you* listen to *me*, Pierre! I won't be dictated to like that! I'll go out with whom I please, and marry whom I please!'

'Ah!' he pounced. 'Then you *are* in love with him!'

'With whom?' she asked bewildered.

He nodded towards the hotel entrance.

'With that conceited Englishman!'

'*Simon Ferguson?*' She threw back her head and laughed. 'Oh, no, Pierre—I can assure you, not *him*!'

There was a stony little silence, then Pierre said quietly: 'Ah—so you *are* in love with someone, *chérie*. I should have guessed, of course. You have been—different—lately. Sort of—how you say?—withdrawn and unapproachable. Not yourself. Not the Suzanne *I* know. What has happened, *chérie*?'

'Nothing has happened, Pierre.'

'You lie, Suzanne.' He regarded her sadly, then shook his head and finished: 'Whoever it is, I hate him, of course. And I will not give you up without a struggle.'

161

She laid an impulsive hand upon his sleeve.

'Pierre, we've been good friends, you and I—just good friends, always. You knew that. I made no promises, offered no hope.'

'I know, I know! I take too much for granted! I think that no one else can possibly steal my Suzanne—and then, one day, I wake up to find she is gone . . .'

'Please, Pierre—don't feel like that!'

'It is true, *chérie*.' Suddenly his sadness gave way to anger again, and in a way she was glad. His sadness was a reproach, but his anger a challenge. 'I tell you this, Suzanne—and do not forget!—I will give you up to no man! Understand? *No man*.'

She answered quietly: 'No man is asking you to, Pierre.'

He stared, a puzzled frown cleaving his handsome forehead.

'I do not understand! You say there is another man'

'I did *not* say so! You assumed it.'

'And you did not deny it. Very well, then, there *is* another man! You love him—yes?'

She was silent a moment, then answered simply: 'Yes.'

His vulnerable young face flinched.

'So—you love each other. And yet you say he does not want you?'

Susan took a deep breath. She was suddenly tired; desperately tired. She wanted to go to her room, to shut the door, to be alone. To cry.

162

'Listen, Pierre—you've made me admit that I am in love. That is true—I'm sorry, really sorry, but it *is* true! But I didn't say that he loves me. The truth is that I mean nothing to him. Nothing at all.'

Pierre gaped.

'*Mon Dieu*, he is *imbécile*, this man!'

A rueful smile touched Susan's mouth.

'No, Pierre, it is I who am mad. Incurably, hopelessly, futilely.' Suddenly she reached up, dropped a kiss upon his cheek, and ran away from him up the stairs.

For a moment he stood looking after her. He could feel the lingering touch of her lips and realised that it was no different from the touch he had known before, when in rare demonstrative moments she had kissed him— lightly and impersonally, without meaning. A kiss of friendship, of companionship, of boy-and-girl affection. Nothing more.

That was the moment when Pierre Dupont grew up. He felt neither anger, nor pique, nor resentment. He didn't even feel sorry for himself. He felt merely an overwhelming sadness and a sense of loss.

He turned to walk out of the hotel and came face to face once more with Simon Ferguson. The man was returning through the front door, an early edition of the evening paper in his hand. He greeted Pierre amiably, but was somewhat surprised when the boy demanded: 'Where is it you take Mademoiselle this evening, M'sieu?'

The Englishman stared.

'As to that, my friend, why should I tell you?'

'Why should you not, M'sieu? Unless it is that you are ashamed and do not wish to reveal where you take her.'

Simon Ferguson laughed.

'Don't be a young fool. Why should I be ashamed of taking her to the Sporting Club? The whole of Monte Carlo will be there and in the midst of such a crowd I can hardly assault her—if that is what's worrying you.'

Pierre gave a mock bow.

'Thank you, M'sieu. The thought had occurred to me—yes.'

'The devil it had! Well, set your mind at rest on that point. Miss Lorrimer isn't my cup of tea at all.'

'Your what?' Pierre echoed in some bewilderment.

'She means nothing to me—is that clearer?'

Pierre said heavily: 'Then it *is* you . . .'

'I don't know what you mean.'

'*You*, M'sieu, are the man—the man to whom she means nothing. Then why did she deny it, I wonder?' Pierre shrugged in bewildered resignation. *Les Anglais* . . . he would never understand them!

The Englishman stared after the French boy as he walked from the hotel. Funny sort of chap, he thought. But then weren't they all?

These French. He would never understand them . . .

CHAPTER SIXTEEN

Despite her doubts, the evening proved enjoyable, with Simon Ferguson completely vindicating Susan's earlier impression of him. He was generous, almost lavish in his entertainment, his behaviour not once overstepping the mark.

Looking back on things later, Susan hadn't the smallest fault to find. Her companion's eyes had admired her without boldness—the kind of admiration which did wonders for a girl's ego. She shone. She sparkled. She knew that even in her simple dress—ballet length, of blue lace—she held her own amongst one of the best-dressed crowds in the world.

She danced tirelessly and had a wonderful time.

Therefore, it was a pity that an incident should occur to mar it.

It happened just before the end of the celebrations. They were sitting at their table, watching the rest of the dancers, a bucket of champagne between them. Simon was replenishing her glass and saying teasingly: 'I mustn't give you too much of this, or your hangover tomorrow will prevent you from working for the worthy Doctor Curtis!'

She didn't like that, nor the tone in which it was said. She didn't like his disparagement of John. Nevertheless, her short nose tilted defiantly as she answered: 'I shan't be working for him much longer, anyway. He's replacing me with a full-time secretary.'

'The devil he is! And why?'

'Because he needs one, I suppose. The clinic is growing rapidly.' She finished miserably: 'I see his point, of course.'

'And is that the only explanation he offered?'

'Oh, he hasn't offered one yet. I mean,' she added hastily, 'he hasn't even told me yet.'

'Then how do you know?'

'Through someone else at the clinic. Someone you don't know. She's married to Doctor Collier—John's assistant—and is a nurse there herself.'

Her companion's eyes betrayed nothing— neither surprise, disappointment, nor speculation. He *was* disappointed, of course. If Susan left the clinic she'd be no further use to him as a source of information. Not that she talked about the place very much, but occasionally he was able to glean something— such as the fact that John's work was achieving success. He hated him for that. Like many people who failed in life, Stephen Foster resented those who didn't.

So he said carefully: 'Collier? Isn't that the

doctor who was mixed up recently in some scandal or other?'

Susan recalled the hints Charlotte had once dropped, but thrust them resolutely aside.

'I know nothing about that,' she answered.

'Then I must be mistaken. I just thought I'd read something about him. Probably I was wrong—though it does seem significant, don't you think, that he should team up with a man with John Curtis's past? I mean, if this fellow Collier had got on a sticky wicket himself, an obscure clinic in Provence would provide a convenient hideaway for him also.'

Susan put down her glass. Somehow, the whole evening had gone flat and no amount of champagne could restore the sparkle.

'You overlook one fact,' she said evenly. 'That the clinic isn't going to remain obscure. I told you the other day that I didn't believe your story about John. I still don't.'

'Because you don't want to,' he said quietly.

She picked up her little diamanté bag, her gossamer stole, and laer long evening gloves.

'Let's go—'

'You're cross, Susan.'

'No. Just disappointed.'

'Naturally. You believed in the clinic. You believed in John Curtis. Obviously, you also believed in Peter Collier—'

She said swiftly: 'How did you know his name was Peter?'

He wasn't caught out.

'I heard old Mrs. Fothergill mention him to your mother. They were talking in the lounge only this evening, whilst I waited for you. The name Peter Collier rang a bell, although I couldn't recall why at the time. Now, I do.'

He was very plausible. So plausible that she believed him—for which he was thankful, because what he said wasn't strictly true. The two women *had* been talking in the lounge. He'd heard their voices as he approached, but they'd kept them low, unfortunately. For a while he had hesitated before descending the stairs. When he appeared they broke off, then continued in normal tones. Their conversation had been inconsequent and when he smiled at them affably, they had both smiled back very promptly.

Mrs. Lorrimer hadn't objected to Susan going out with him, either; so far as the girl's mother was concerned, he felt confident. As for the old woman, she was no danger at all. She was too old and too garrulous to be anything more than a tiresome gossip.

He tried to persuade Susan to dance again, but she said she was tired and pleaded to go home. He didn't try to dissuade her. It seemed unlikely that he was going to learn anything more about the situation at St. Maria, so he might as well call it a day. Besides, if they left now he could go on to the Casino after escorting Susan back to the Villa d'Este. Since his meeting with Catherine yesterday he had fresh funds with which to gamble. He hadn't been doing too well the last few days, but another go at the tables might change his luck.

Back at the hotel, Susan thanked him, said goodnight, and went straight up to her room. She told him she'd had a wonderful evening, which was true up to a point. Therefore it was illogical to fling herself upon her bed and weep her heart out, which was what she did the minute her door was closed.

On the other side of her bedroom wall, Ruth Lorrimer lay awake. Charlotte had given her much to think about. There was no denying the evidence of those press cuttings— the man calling himself Simon Ferguson bore an unmistable likeness to Doctor Stephen Foster. And, of course, there was also the report featuring that nice young Doctor Collier, his erstwhile partner.

Both Ruth and Charlotte felt sorry for Peter Collier, and agreed that the thing to do was to get rid of Stephen Foster.

But how? Without just cause, a hotel proprietor couldn't ask a guest to leave and, so far, this man had given no cause for complaint. Ruth hadn't particularly liked his attentions to her daughter, but since they had been in no way objectionable, she couldn't make that an excuse. And if she did ask him to go, what good would it serve? He would merely find another hotel and remain in Monte Carlo without the advantage of being under their

169

eye.

What puzzled Ruth was how he had come to the Villa d'Este. Not by mere coincidence, she was convinced. Charlotte insisted that Catherine must have sent him and it seemed the only explanation. She knew the place; had stayed here herself. She had, in fact, preceded his arrival.

If it were true that Catherine had sent him, it confirmed Charlotte's suspicion that she was, in some way, involved with him.

Ruth tossed restlessly in her bed. She didn't want it to be true. Not because she particularly liked Catherine, although she felt there was some fundamental good in her, but because it suggested that, behind John's back, a certain amount of intrigue was going on which might ultimately prove damaging to the clinic.

Ruth's thoughts diverted to John and Susan.

Was it true, as Charlotte suggested, that they were in love—or, at any rate, attracted by each other?

A sound from beyond her bedroom wall cut into Ruth's thoughts. At once, she was alert. It was the sound of someone crying, and it came from Susan's room.

She was out of bed in a flash. Not since Joseph's death had she heard Susan cry, and now the sound held the same, duality of grief, the same terrible sense of loss.

But when she tapped on Susan's door, there was immediate silence. She tapped again and called: 'Susan! Darling, are you awake?' When she turned the door handle it yielded. Susan always slept with her curtains drawn back and a shaft of moonlight revealed her young figure prostrate upon the bed, her lace dress a crumpled heap, a damp handkerchief knotted in one hand . . .

Ruth gathered her up as if she were still a child.

'Susan—darling—what has happened? Didn't you enjoy yourself tonight?'

Susan gulped and nodded.

'I had a wonderful time!' she wailed.

Ruth checked a smile.

'Then what has gone wrong?' she asked gently.

'Everything! just everything!'

'Tell me—'

'I'm leaving the clinic, that's all!'

'But *why*?'

Susan pulled herself together.

'Because I've got other work—nearer home, too. That's why.'

'Susan, you're lying to me . . .'

'No. It's true.'

Ruth regarded her daughter in bewilderment. She said slowly:

'If leaving the clinic makes you as unhappy as this, Susan, there must be a reason.' When the girl didn't answer, she said gently: 'You love him, don't you? You love Doctor Curtis.'

Susan closed her eyes and relaxed against

171

her mother's shoulder with a deep sigh. Now that the words were uttered, now the truth was out, it was almost a relief.

'Yes, mother. I do love him. So you see, I *must* go!'

'It seems the most illogical reason I ever heard!'

'Surely *you* understand?'

'If he didn't care about you, darling, I would.'

Susan said with unaccustomed bitterness: 'Well, he doesn't care about me, you can be sure of that.' She sat up and dried her eyes. 'Don't look at me like that, mother, I'm not going to be fool enough to cry any more. I can't think what made me!'

'I can. Something has happened, something you are keeping back . . .'

She waited, but Susan said nothing. She wasn't going to reveal Catherine's information—the information that John was planning to dismiss her—any more than she was going to reveal the ugly story about John which Simon Ferguson had told her. She wasn't even going to think about it, let alone believe it. The scar on John's wrist must have some other explanation.

She leaned across and kissed her mother. 'Go back to bed now. I'm sorry I disturbed you. I'm all right, I promise.'

But Ruth's anxiety, as she returned to her room, was deeper than before.

CHAPTER SEVENTEEN

John was pleased with his new little patient; Sally Beaumont's progress was more than satisfactory and she was very soon transferred from her isolated ward to a larger one, with other children. Her mother was naturally delighted, and said so.

'I shall never forget all you've done for Sally, Doctor Curtis.'

'She isn't better yet—not completely,' he warned.

'But she is going to be! I know she is going to be!'

John knew that, too. Sally's case was one of his most successful.

Diana Beaumont still remained at Eze-sur-Mer, driving up to St. Maria every day to see her daughter. Not even the most tempting film contract could lure her away. But, as Catherine said, money meant little to her—she had so much of it. Not all the money in the world, however, could buy health and happiness and she frankly confessed to Catherine that she would have given all she possessed to see Sally enjoying life like other children.

'You're going to see her doing that in the very near future, Mrs. Beaumont . . . Think of that!'

They were having tea together in the staff sitting-room—a custom they had fallen into as a result of Diana's frequent visits. Now she leaned forward confidentially and said: 'Nurse—you can advise me; help me, even! Doctor Curtis is a reserved man. When I try to discuss fees with him, he seems to avoid the subject—'

Catherine smiled.

'That's typical of John! For one thing, he's no businessman—he's a doctor, first, last and foremost—and for another, money, or the discussion of it, embarrasses him. The account will be rendered in the usual way, so don't give it another thought.'

'I certainly shall! I've given it plenty of thought already and I know precisely what I want to do. I want to help this clinic because it deserves helping. I want to help Doctor Curtis, because he deserves it, too. And the simplest way for me to do that is to help financially. Why not?'

'Because John is a proud man. He hates charity.'

'This wouldn't be charity—it would be business. Doesn't he realise that pride and business don't mix?'

'But the clinic isn't merely a business to him. It's his whole life.'

As Catherine uttered the words she realised, bleakly, that they were true. Nothing was so important to John as medicine.

174

Nothing—and no one. Certainly not herself.

'He is a dedicated man,' she said softly. 'You must understand that to men such as he the work, and the results of that work, mean everything.'

'I respect him for that, but why shouldn't I pay more when I can so easily afford it? Believe me, Sally's health is more precious than wealth. I've been successful, Nurse. I can't deny that. So I may as well put my money to good account. I'm a widow, you know, and Sally is all I have. Just as medicine is the chief thing in the Doctor's life, so Sally is, in mine.'

Suddenly and unaccountably, Catherine felt an envy for this woman. Not for her beauty, her face, or her success, but for her motherhood. A woman who didn't experience that, she thought suddenly, was like an empty shell . . .

'Is it true, Nurse—and I've heard it is—that Doctor Curtis treats poor children absolutely free?'

'In some cases. Others he judges upon their parents' means, charging what he thinks they can afford.'

'Then why doesn't he charge me what *I* can afford?'

'You must put that argument to him—not to me,' Catherine smiled.

'But you agree?'

'Yes—I do.'

'Couldn't *you* argue with him, then?'

'I've tried.'

The sharp peal of the telephone cut into the moment. Then it ceased. Someone had taken it in another part of the house. A sense of uneasiness—illogical and acute—touched Catherine's heart, and was confirmed a moment later when John's head appeared round the door.

'Someone for you, Catherine. He wouldn't give his name . . .'

There was a puzzled look in his eyes, however, and, when Catherine picked up the receiver, she knew why. Stephen Foster's voice echoed down the line.

'I've been unlucky again, Catherine. I've lost every penny. In fact, my sweet, I fear I shall be unable to pay my hotel bill . . .'

She couldn't answer. Her mouth went dry. Across the room, John and Diana Beaumont were talking in low voices. Beneath their conversation John observed Catherine's silence and, tactfully, opened the tall French windows and led Diana out into the garden. But not until he had covertly observed the nurse's face, and the stillness of it.

He wondered why the man named Ferguson, staying—as Susan had admitted the other day—at the Villa d'Este, should be telephoning Peter's wife. For that was who it was. He'd recognised the voice, even though the man had refused to give his name. And the voice had troubled him today, as it had done the previous time—troubled him with a vague sense of familiarity. He felt that in some way he should be able to identify it, but could not.

When they returned, Catherine had hung up. She was pale, but composed. John said goodbye to Diana Beaumont and went back to his work. Susan was coming this afternoon and he was looking forward to that . . .

When he had gone, Catherine said: 'I'll see you to your car, Mrs. Beaumont . . .'

'Not until I've enlisted your aid, Nurse. You haven't forgotten what we were discussing, surely?'

'No—I haven't forgotten'

'Well, then—won't you help me?' She put her hand upon Catherine's sleeve and said urgently: 'I've thought the whole thing out! Why shouldn't I make a donation to the clinic, as a mark of my appreciation? It could do with funds, surely?'

'It could, indeed.'

'Very well, then! I will give the cheque to you, Nurse, and *you* will pay it into the clinic's account for me! It's as easy as that!'

As easy as that! thought Catherine. So terribly, terribly easy . . .

'No!' she said sharply. 'I can't do it!'

Diana Beaumont didn't press the subject.

'Very well—I'll say no more about it. Not now, at any rate. Meanwhile, I'll say nothing to Doctor Curtis, either, but I'd like you to think it over. Will you do that?'

*　　*　　*

Susan arrived as Diana departed. The big, high-powered car swept past her on the drive, but Susan scarcely noticed it. This afternoon she was going to tell John that she was leaving, and she was going to get it in before he did. Instead of satisfying her, the thought depressed her.

She was almost glad he wasn't in the office—it postponed the moment for a while, at least. She set to work and continued steadily until the door opened and Peter entered.

'Sorry to interrupt,' he said pleasantly. 'I was looking for John.'

'I haven't seen him yet. Perhaps he's in the lab.'

'I'll go and see.'

But he lingered, glancing over her shoulder and saying with interest: 'How's the book going? Pretty well, I see. You're up to Chapter Thirteen . . .'

'An unlucky number!' she said lightly. 'And I think it's going to be.'

Sensing something in her tone, his amusement died. It was unusual for Susan to be anything but cheerful.

'Why, Susan? What do you mean?'

'Simply that I may not finish it. In fact, I'm pretty sure I won't finish it, unless Doctor Curtis can write the remaining chapters in a

178

week, and providing I can type them in that time.'

'I hope that doesn't mean what it seems to imply—that you won't be here to finish them? Are you going on holiday—is that it? And since when has John been 'Doctor Curtis' to you?'

She ignored the last remark.

'I'm not going on holiday, Peter. I'm leaving.'

'Susan! No!'

'I've agreed to do more work for the Consulate.'

'But, good heavens, why?'

Suddenly she found it difficult to speak.

'Ask Catherine!' she choked. 'She'll tell you why! And now, *please*, Peter—let me get on!' When he reached the door she called after him: 'And don't say anything to John about it! I want to tell him myself.'

'All right,' he answered uneasily.

But he didn't like it. John wasn't going to like it, either—he was certain of that. Of all the things to happen, he thought glumly, just when everything was going so well and John was hoping to employ her full-time!

Catherine's trim figure disappeared ahead of him into one of the wards. She walked swiftly, and he hurried to catch up with her. When he entered the ward she was stooping over the cot of a sleeping child—a very young child that had kicked its bed-covers off. For a

179

moment Peter stood there, watching his wife. She ought to be doing that to a child of her own, he thought, and forgot all about Susan and what it was he wanted to speak to Catherine about.

He still wasn't perfectly happy about his relationship with his wife, although it had improved, he felt, since coming to St. Maria. At times it was almost happy. Their rooms at the top of the house had an atmosphere of home which they had never known in Harley Street. There were even times when he thought she was learning to love him, in the way that he loved her. Then a shutter seemed to come down between them, and she was nervy and irritable again. But even at such times there was still hope, for she sought refuge from such moods in work—not in gaiety any more. And, once with the children, she softened. That was why he knew that the best thing for Catherine was to have a child.

She looked up from the cot and saw him. Was she pleased to see him? He couldn't tell. But there was a change in her expression; a sort of relaxation which, even at this distance, he detected. Had she been feeling tense about something—a mood which seemed to touch her too often of late? A mood he couldn't account for. He had hoped, when they came to St. Maria, that they would at least find peace together. Yet sometimes he thought she was more nervy than ever . . .

All the same, she didn't avoid him, as once she would have avoided him. She didn't brush him aside impatiently, or turn away from his kisses. She even seemed to draw comfort from them, which was pleasing at the same time as it was worrying, for why, he wondered, should his wife need comforting? Especially in such a place as this . . .

She attended to the needs of one or two other small patients, then walked down the ward towards him. He thought how beautiful she was—even that brittle quality seemed to have lessened slightly. Was that the result of nursing these children? He thought it must be.

'Are you looking for me?' she asked outside the ward. 'For anything special?'

'Must it be for something special?' he smiled.

She slipped her arm through his, spontaneously and of her own free will. He felt that she clung to it in a needful sort of way.

'Is anything wrong, Catherine?'

'Nothing!' she jerked. 'Absolutely nothing! Why?'

'Because if there were,' he said slowly, 'you'd tell me, wouldn't you?'

For a fleeting moment her eyes scanned his face—the glance was almost questioning, as if seeking assurance. *And if I did tell you?* she wondered. *What would you do, Peter?*

What would any husband do, in the circumstances? She thought she knew, and dropped his arm abruptly. It was useless to hope for help from any quarter. She had to help herself, and the situation was becoming desperate. She had to dispose of Stephen once and for all. Somehow . . . *somehow* . . .

There must be a way! There *had* to be a way! He couldn't go on for ever, torturing her, frightening her, turning the screw . . . She had only written a few of those foolish notes to him—but how many? Dear God, how many? If only she could remember! But there couldn't be many more. 'A couple or so', he said, and to the best of her recollection he must be speaking the truth this time.

Of course, she'd been a fool. She'd been the worst fool on earth! She should have called his bluff that first day they met. Would he really have dared to spread scandal about the clinic, to tell lies about John's reputation, to undermine, once again, Peter's chances of a decent career?

Yes, he would indeed! A man like that would stop at nothing! It was no use deluding herself on that point. Until those damaging little notes were out of his possession and finally destroyed, he had her completely in his power; take that power away, and his other threats could be fought.

She looked at Peter's trusting face and was ashamed. In the old days, it had irritated her. He had been too slavish, too gullible, too devoted altogether. But now she needed—and wanted—his devotion. Now it was her only comfort, for she knew she could never win it from John now that Susan Lorrimer had come into his life . . .

That she was selfish, Catherine knew. That she used people for her own ends, she acknowledged. That she wanted Peter, now, because there was no hope of having John— this, she feared, was also true. But at least I've *tried* to help him, haven't I? At least, I've helped him to get a new start here, and worked beside him, and enjoyed the work . . .

A sudden flame of determination shot through her. She'd make one last bid to dispose of Stephen Foster, one last attempt to ensure that this new-found security at St. Maria should not be shattered altogether.

But how? She hadn't any money left. Not a penny. Peter had given her a portion of their capital and the rest he had invested in the clinic, so it would be impossible to get any more from him.

But if she could borrow it? If, in time, she could pay it back? The clinic was progressing. John had said only this morning that the whole situation would have to be reviewed. He'd be taking Peter into full partnership and she herself would receive the salary her work deserved—he'd told her that. So if she could get a loan from somewhere, she was confident of repaying it.

Peter said suddenly: 'Did you know Susan

was leaving?'

'Is she?' she answered carefully. 'When?'

'End of next week, I gather. She told me just now. John doesn't know yet, but she said that you did. At least, when I asked her why she was going, she told me you knew . . .'

'But, of course! John's getting a new secretary, isn't he? A full-time one. I heard him say so.'

'It was to be Susan—naturally—providing she would agree to come!'

Catherine looked away. Guilt moved her uncomfortably, but she really couldn't worry about Susan just now. She had a heavier problem on her mind.

'I daresay she could be persuaded to remain,' she said absently. 'Peter, I must go—there's something I've got to attend to at once . . .'

'I thought you were off duty this afternoon, darling.'

'So I am. I'm going down to Monte Carlo beach for a swim, so I must hurry!'

She blew him a kiss and hurried away down the corridor. Reaching the staff sitting-room, she closed the door carefully and picked up the telephone.

Diana Beaumont had not arrived back at Eze-sur-Mer, so Catherine left a message. An urgent one.

'Tell Madame Beaumont that Nurse Collier has thought the matter over and agrees to her

184

suggestion. Yes, yes—she will know what I mean! Tell her, also, that we can settle things when she comes to see her daughter tomorrow . . .'

*   *   *

Susan was alone in the office when John entered. He looked at her shining head and a feeling of pleasure ran through him—a pleasure so intense that, for the: moment, he could not speak.

Susan continued typing steadily.

He came and stood behind her, looking down at her work. But he scarcely saw it. All he really saw was the gleam of her hair and again he felt the urge to put out his hand and stroke it. He wondered how she would react if he did, and decided not to try.

'You've been busy, I see. It was good of you to continue the work at home, Susan.'

She forced herself to look up at him. Her heart was beating wildly—so wildly that he must surely hear? It became even more uncontrolled when she saw his eyes smiling down at her. They were deep-set eyes; grey, flecked with green. They were keen and intelligent and passionate and disturbing. She turned away swiftly and went on with her work.

'There's still a lot to do,' she said briskly.

'It will all get done in time. Personally, I'm more than satisfied with the progress of this book.'

'I'm glad.'

It all sounded so stilted and unnatural. What was the matter between them? Why couldn't they achieve the pleasant companionship they had known? Why had it all become personal and out-of-hand and disturbing?

It was her own fault, of course. She shouldn't have fallen in love with him. It had made her self-conscious in his presence; aware of his every glance, his every movement; every shadow and nuance in his voice. Did he sense her reaction? Even more appalling was the possibility that he might guess the reason for it. Her cheeks flamed at the thought and she stooped lower over her work.

She's avoiding me, thought John. Why? Does she know how I feel about her? Is she embarrassed by it? And how *do* I feel about her?

He couldn't put a name to the effect she had upon him, because, of course, it couldn't be love.

But why not? *Why not?* Because of twelve years' difference between them? But that was nothing! Indeed, it was a comfortable margin; a pleasant margin. He was old enough to take care of her; to love her as a man, not a boy; to appreciate her youth, without taking it for granted . . .

He stood silently, pondering upon the

186

realisation in a kind of bemused wonder. It couldn't be possible that he loved her; it couldn't be true! For years he had loved Catherine and, because of her, had bothered with no other women. Catherine, he had thought, embodied his ideal—the kind of woman, and the only kind, that he could ever care for. Yet here he was, standing behind Susan Lorrimer's chair, and longing to gather her up and hold her close . . .

He said: 'Susan, I've something to tell you—'

Here it is, she thought. He's going to say, as kindly and politely as he can, that he's sorry, but I have to go. And I'll make a fool of myself. I'll break down and cry or something equally silly, and then he'll be embarrassed and even more glad to get rid of me . . .

Her head went up.

'And I have something to tell you, Doctor! I must ask you to accept my notice. I shall be leaving at the end of next week.'

It was out. Done. Finished with. She'd forestalled him and saved her own face. And all for the sake of her stupid pride—the pride which had assured her that if she did this she would feel triumphant and satisfied. And she wasn't. She wanted to cry, just the same.

There was silence in the little room. He was looking at her in a stunned kind of way. Then he said: 'I think I must have misunderstood—'

'There's nothing to misunderstand, Doctor. I've agreed to do more work at the Consulate.

That means I can no longer work for you.'

'But why?' he managed to get out. '*Why*, in the name of heaven?'

'Why not? The Consulate is nearer home. Financially, I shall be better off, because I shall have no travelling expenses . . .'

'I would have paid your fares—' he began stiffly.

'*Please*, Doctor!'

Suddenly, he was angry. He was glad of that. Anger was a safety valve against emotion and at all costs he had to hide how he felt about this. She was leaving him and the decision was her own, which meant that she was leaving him because she wanted to. *She wanted to.*

So he had been deluding himself when he imagined that the work interested her, that the clinic meant something to her, that she found the work absorbing because it was *his* work, *his* life . . .

He said slowly: 'I thought you were interested in the book and that you liked the work here . . .'

'A good secretary is always interested in her work, no matter what.'

'Which means that working at the Consulate will mean as much to you as the job here?'

She was sitting with her back to him, so he didn't see her face—nor her slim hands, nervously clenching and unclenching in her lap.

'Of course!' she lied.

He took a deep breath, turned on his heel, and moved towards the door.

Her voice followed him.

'Have you no dictation for me this afternoon, Doctor?'

'None whatever. When you've finished that batch, you can call it a day. I'm sure the Consulate will be glad to employ you without waiting a further week.'

She sat very still. Her face was still, too. Stunned and rigid and disbelieving. She hadn't expected him to take it like that. She hadn't expected anger. After all, he'd been about to dismiss her, so why should he resent being forestalled?

For a moment of passionate antagonism they regarded each other. And in that moment he realised how deeply he did love her; that the emotions she aroused in him were intense and real and nothing he had ever felt before matched up with them. This was more than the physical desire which, in Catherine's case, he had confused with love. This was of the mind and the heart and the body, too. But Susan didn't know that. She couldn't feel it. There had never been any response on her part and he'd been a fool to imagine it.

He turned away abruptly.

'You can leave immediately, as far as I am concerned.'

Without a backward glance, he walked from the room.

CHAPTER EIGHTEEN

Of course, he'd behaved like a fool—John knew that. He'd been piqued and hurt and angry—disillusioned, too. So he'd hit back at Susan, behaving as a man in love too often behaves. And all because of his stupid pride; because he didn't want her to know that he was hurt.

He didn't see her before she left. He didn't go near the office until later that evening—when he was sure, quite sure, that she had gone. When he finally entered he saw the neatly typed manuscript placed within a folder on her desk, and that was all.

He pulled open the drawers of the desk—he didn't know why—and saw that everything had been left in meticulous order. From the top right hand drawer, in which she had kept her handbag, a faint perfume emerged. It came from a handkerchief, a simple one of plain linen. For a moment he stood looking at it, then slowly picked it up.

It wasn't an expensive handkerchief, but it was hemstitched and clean and there was a fragrance about it which, for ever more, he would associate with Susan; a delicate fragrance, like that of wild flowers. He didn't know what the perfume was, but nothing could have personified her more perfectly. He lifted the scrap of linen to his face and the fragrance was like a breath reaching his heart . . .

A sound from the door made him conceal the handkerchief quickly. He thrust it within an inside pocket of his jacket and the gesture was oddly significant. It told Peter a lot, as he stood there looking at the man whom he valued as a friend above all others.

Peter closed the door and crossed the room.

'John—you're not going to let her go, are you?' As if in explanation, he added: 'Susan told me this afternoon that she was leaving.'

'She isn't leaving—she has left.'

'And you *let* her? You let her go, just like that?'

John turned away.

'She wanted to go. She told me so.'

'But for what reason? Good heavens, man, there must *be* a reason! This job meant a lot to Susan!'

'I thought so, too. Apparently I was wrong.'

'Not only the job—*you* meant a lot to her, John.'

'This time it is you who are wrong.'

'I'm not. I'm quite sure I'm not. Why don't you go to her and ask her point blank what's behind all this?'

John shrugged wearily.

'What's the use? She told me, anyway. She'll be better off working for the British Consulate and the work there will interest her just as much as this. She told me that, too.'

'I can't believe it—and I certainly can't understand it. There's more behind this than we know about, John.'

'I wish there were!'

'Did she know you were hoping to employ her full-time?'

'I didn't get a chance to mention it. I was just about to, when she sprang this upon me.'

'And you didn't even tell her *then*?'

'Of course not. I have some pride.'

'Pride! Good heavens, man, you can't afford to have pride when you're in love!'

John stood very still, his back turned. Peter moved uncomfortably.

'Sorry if I've said the wrong thing. I didn't mean to touch on something which obviously means a great deal to you.'

'How did you know?' John's voice was taut.

'You forget I've been in love myself.'

'No one else knows, I hope?'

'Unfortunately, no. I say unfortunately because I wish it had been equally obvious to Susan.'

'Thank heaven it wasn't!'

Peter watched John as he walked from the room. He was worried about him, but he was equally worried about Catherine. She had returned from Monte Carlo looking pale and tired—not in the least invigorated by her swim, nor rested by her afternoon upon the beach. She hadn't said much, either; merely that she was tired and she hoped he wouldn't mind if she went straight to bed after cooking his supper. Because he loved her, he'd packed her off at once, insisting that he'd cook supper instead. When he'd taken her tray into the bedroom she'd looked at it for a long moment, then burst into tears.

He hoped she didn't realise how disturbed he was by those tears. He'd put his arms about her and she'd subsided against him, sobbing: 'Oh, Peter, *why* are you so good to me?'

'Because I love you, of course—why else?'

When he went to bed she appeared to be asleep, so he undressed very quietly and slipped into bed beside her. He didn't touch her. He listened for a while to her regular breathing then, finally, slept. After he had been asleep for some time Catherine slipped out of bed, donned a dressing-gown, and went out on to the balcony.

Far below lay the lights of Monte Carlo, outlining the harbour like a garland. She could see the Palace of Monaco softly illuminated, and the Casino beyond—ornate and flood-lit. Well, she thought wryly, at least Stephen wouldn't be there tonight, gambling away his last penny, because until she let him have some more money he hadn't a penny left to gamble with. He'd made that quite clear during their meeting this afternoon, and his attitude had been far from pleasant. In fact, she had found it difficult to convince him that shortly, within a few days if her plans worked out, she would be able to help him for the last time.

Beneath her fear of him, contempt stirred. Once she had actually admired his gay bravado, his sophistication and wit. She had made allowances for his excesses because, she thought, a woman of the world should do so. She smiled bitterly, feeling nothing but contempt for herself. A woman of the world wouldn't have been so naïve and trusting as to write a series of compromising little notes to such a man as he. Nor to any man, for that matter.

She didn't deserve a husband like Peter— she acknowledged that now. If she realised this too late, she had only herself to blame. But of one thing she was equally sure—that she had obtained most of those stupid notes from Stephen and destroyed them, and that the one he had flaunted before her today was certainly the last. It even said so. '. . . *This is the last time I shall write to you, Stephen—it's time we stopped this affair of ours. As far as I am concerned, it has stopped already. Had I known you were carrying on with that society girl I certainly wouldn't have cheapened myself with you . . .*'

The final note of all—and the most damning! That, of course, was why he had saved it until last. Those decisive words could mean anything; they could be interpreted to mean the very worst and he, of course, would

194

declare that they did, if need be. But even a flirtation after marriage could be cheap and sordid, and by that time it had seemed so, even to a woman with as light a conscience as her own.

She wasn't sorry she had submitted to Stephen's blackmail; any price was worth his silence. But now her reason had changed; originally she had wanted to conceal the truth because it threatened not only her security, but the clinic, too. She didn't want John to know what kind of a woman she was and, equally, she didn't want anything to disrupt things here. As for Peter, it was essential that he should remain in ignorance because if the truth came out he would certainly leave her—and, as Stephen had pointed out, if Peter left the clinic John would have to know why. He wouldn't forgive her. He wouldn't employ her, either. So she was glad she had submitted to Stephen's threats because in so doing she had, at least, averted all that.

But now she was even more glad for a different reason—or an additional one. And that reason was simply and solely Peter himself. At the beginning, he had been important only in so far as he affected her employment here, but now he was important for a reason which seemed more deeply personal and which she could not define.

But at last, thank God, the end was in sight. She had one last step to take—and it couldn't fail. Why should it? Within a day or two she would have that final incriminating note in her hands and after that Stephen could prove nothing; after that, what would it avail him to whisper and slander? The clinic had proved itself, and although damaging tongues could always undermine an organisation or a cause, he wouldn't be able to back his scandal-mongering with any sort of proof. Not any more.

The lights of St. Maria had long since been extinguished, for the village kept early hours. From a distant ward there came the faint cry of a child, and then silence. The night nurse had soothed it quickly. Catherine's training made her temporarily alert and then, once more, she returned to her thoughts.

The clinic had come to mean a lot to her—not merely as a refuge and a fresh start, not merely because it enabled her to be near John, but as a nurse; a nurse who really cared for her work and for the patients beneath her care. That, at least, could be placed to her credit, she thought wearily, if nothing else could.

A sound from below attracted her attention; the sound of footsteps upon gravel. She leaned over the balcony and saw John's tall figure walking in the shadowy garden. He was fully dressed and she wondered what had kept him up so late. Had he been working on that book of his, and come out for a last stroll before turning in, or was he, like herself, unable to sleep?

Something in his stance—the set of his shoulders and the restless movements of his hands—told her that he was disturbed about something. She wanted to call out to him, but dare not because of waking Peter. She wanted to go down to him, but instinct urged her not to. He wouldn't welcome her, or anyone, she felt. He was walking alone in the garden because he wanted to *be* alone; because something was on his mind.

Could it be Susan? Catherine felt a pang of envy and regret, knowing that she guessed rightly. As far as John was concerned, he would never love herself again—she had to accept that fact, deeply as it hurt a woman accustomed to male adulation. She had made herself useful to him and he appreciated that—but as a woman he looked upon her merely as the wife of his best friend. And maybe, after all, it was a good thing . . .

But it hurt. She had thrown away a good man when she turned John down. Why had she deluded herself that he would be easy to win back? From the moment that Susan Lorrimer entered this house she, Catherine Collier, hadn't stood a chance. That was an ironical and bitter thought. She had beauty, wit, and everything to offer a man—and all he saw was a slip of a girl who appeared, on the surface, to be ordinary and uninteresting. But was she? In this rare moment of honesty

197

Catherine had to admit that Susan, when one really got to know her, was attractive, lively, and intelligent. When she became a woman her beauty would be serene and lovely; the sort of beauty some girls achieve only through maturity and love.

John's solitary figure disappeared from view and for a brief moment Catherine felt sorry for him. Then it was lost beneath a returning tide of self-pity; her own problems again absorbed her. Stephen Foster still lurked like a threatening shadow—she hadn't disposed of him yet. And this afternoon his mood had been particularly threatening and ugly, not caring who saw them together; even insisting that they should have their talk in the lounge of the Villa d'Este—in a discreet and sheltered corner, of course. What harm could it do? he taunted. Who, in this modest little establishment, knew anything about them? What did it matter that the garrulous old Mrs. Fothergill worked at the clinic—was there any law which said that Doctor Collier's wife shouldn't have tea with an old acquaintance from England? Everyone here knew him as Simon Ferguson, anyway, and beyond that— nothing.

As for the two women—old Charlotte and her friend, Ruth Lorrimer—he had them eating out of his hand. Or so he declared. Flatter women past the age of forty, he said, and you could pull the wool over their eyes with ease.

Catherine hoped he was right. She hoped, quite desperately, that he was right. Because old Charlotte Fothergill had certainly observed them. Across the lounge she had waved a piece of her eternal sewing and called: 'Welcome back to the Villa d'Este, Mrs. Collier! It's nice to see you here again . . .' But that was all. And there was nothing whatsoever to be feared from *that*!

There might have been nothing to fear from it, but Catherine was underrating Charlotte's intelligence when overlooking the fact that there was much to be gleaned. It meant, the old lady decided, that these two had travelled separately on the autobus from St. Maria that day because they (or only Catherine?) were afraid of being seen together and that now things had so developed that Catherine was becoming reckless and Stephen Foster over-confident.

But what things? He had some hold over her, of course. Catherine was too shrewd and too circumspect to mix with a man so recently exposed to disgrace, unless for a reason—and that reason could only be an unpleasant one. Besides, the girl was obviously nearing the end of her tether; that was apparent in so many ways; from the look of strain about her, the shadows beneath her eyes, the nervous movements of her hands, the thinly-suppressed anxiety which gave vent to flashes of temper and irritability. Oh, there were a dozen indications that the wife of young Doctor Collier was in a state of nervous tension these days!

After Catherine's meeting with Stephen Foster in the lounge of the Villa d'Este, Charlotte had lost no time in reporting to Ruth Lorrimer. She found her in her private sitting-room, checking accounts.

'Put those on one side, Ruth—what I've got to tell you is much more important!'

'Nothing could be more important than our bread and butter,' Ruth had protested mildly. But she obeyed, just the same. Something about Charlotte's expression made her.

'They've been having tea together downstairs—quite openly, my dear, which speaks for itself, I think . . .'

'*Who* have been having tea, Charlotte?'

'Why, the man who calls himself Ferguson, and Catherine Collier, of course! I *told* you they knew each other, didn't I?'

'Since the press cuttings, which you so fortuitously cherished, prove beyond a shadow of doubt that Peter Collier was his partner in Harley Street, it is only logical to assume that they know one another, my dear!'

'I also told you that they'd been meeting—'

'Mere assumption,' Ruth reminded her.

'But not now! He brought her in here as bold as brass this afternoon . . .'

'Which means they have nothing to hide.'

'Which means that they believe *we* believe they have nothing to hide!'

'And are we so sure, now?'

'We're sure of one thing,' Charlotte said practically, 'and that is that Catherine's husband doesn't know they're meeting. Nor does anyone at the clinic, since she's so careful to meet this man away from there.'

'Did you hear what they discussed? I'm perfectly sure you'd eavesdrop quite blatantly if you could.'

'Wouldn't you, in this case? After all, the man *is* paying attention to your daughter, and he's not the kind you want running after Susan.'

'I admit all that!' Ruth sighed. 'Well, Charlotte, did you hear anything?'

'Hardly a word, although I strained my ears to bursting point! I sat with my back to them, too, but only because I obtained a perfect view in the wall mirror opposite. What my ears couldn't catch, my eyes observed, and you can take it from me that unhappy young woman is afraid of that man. *I* think he's blackmailing her!'

'Nonsense!'

'It isn't nonsense, Ruth. It happens, you know. It happens far more frequently than people realise—and far more frequently than it need, if people only had sense enough to go to the police—and courage enough, as well. After all, names in such cases are never

201

published—except the names of the criminals, of course.'

Ruth smiled. 'You seem to know a lot about such things, Charlotte.'

'You forget that until I occupied my time at the clinic I read an unlimited amount of detective fiction!'

'But if it's true about Catherine Collier and this man—and we don't know that it is!—what can *we* do about it?'

For once, Charlotte was at a loss—but not discouraged.

'I'll think of something,' she declared confidently. 'I *always* think of something!'

Their conversation was curtailed by Susan, who entered the room at that moment. Her eyes bore unmistakable evidence of recent tears.

Ruth was unable to refrain from asking what was wrong.

'Nothing,' Susan answered casually, 'except that I've left the clinic.'

The two women stared.

Susan said dully: 'Don't look like that—as if you can't believe it!'

'Well, *I* can't for one!' Charlotte exclaimed, and Ruth said helplessly: 'My dear, I didn't really believe you'd go through with it.'

'*Why* have you left, my girl? Taken leave of your senses?'

'I have left, Charlotte, because John doesn't want, or need, me any more.'

'Rubbish! That much I know isn't true.'

Susan flung herself down in a chair.

'It isn't rubbish. He's engaging a full-time secretary in my place. He has every right, if he wants to, and I've got other work to fill the gap, so why should I worry?'

'Because you love him!' the old lady retorted crossly. 'You know very well you love him! And if *he* doesn't know he loves you, the man's a fool!'

'Charlotte, please!'

'Sorry, Ruth—but I mean it. It's obvious to anyone with half an eye that he loves this daughter of yours and I know perfectly well that he *was* planning to engage a full-time secretary—Susan herself, if she'd agree to accept the job! He told me so!'

'You heard wrongly, or misunderstood,' Susan's voice trembled. Charlotte's imagination could sometimes be amusing, but right now her romantic suppositions merely hurt. 'You're wrong about everything, Charlotte.'

'All right—then tell me this! Did he *tell* you to go?'

'No. But only because I gave my notice in first.'

'And you did that—why? Because he let you know he was engaging someone in your place?'

'N-no,' Susan admitted reluctantly. 'It wasn't he who told me.'

'Then who did?

'That doesn't matter.'

'On the contrary, my dear, I think it does. Was it Nurse Collier? Ah—I thought so! No, you needn't answer—I can see it in your eyes. That young woman wants every man for herself, and she's jealous—mark my words, she's jealous! She was jealous because John was going to ask you to work for him full-time, and she knew what *that* would eventually lead to. Do you think I haven't seen the way she looks at you when you're unaware of it? Do you think I can't guess why she told you he was engaging a secretary in your place, before he had a chance to say a word? To get you out of the way, my dear—once and for all. To make you go of your own accord—and then he'd believe he himself meant nothing to you. I may be old, Susan child, but I'm not senile. And my eyesight is remarkably good!'

'So is your sense of romance, Charlotte—but don't dream up dreams for me, please! He didn't care in the least—in fact, he told me to go at once! He didn't even want me to work the week out!'

'Ah—he was angry, was he? Good! Very good! A nice healthy sign of a man in love, if ever I saw one!'

'You're talking nonsense!' Susan sobbed, and ran from the room.

CHAPTER NINETEEN

Pierre was in a black mood. Arriving at the clinic to find no sign of Susan made him wonder if her absence was due to their quarrel. Not that their exchange could really be classed as such; she had even kissed him when they parted, although in rather an unsatisfactory manner. A rather sad little kiss, but not one of finality or parting. Or so he had thought. Nevertheless he had not seen, or heard, from her since. By the greatest will-power he had decided to wait until they met at the clinic this afternoon.

At first he was not perturbed by her non-appearance. The autobus from Monte Carlo was sometimes late, and such was the case today. From the wide window of the children's playroom, in which he held the modelling class, he could see the wrought iron gates at the foot of the drive. Passengers alighted before reaching this point, so he had to allow a lapse of time, after the bus had driven by, for Susan to climb the hill. After a while he saw one or two people pass the gates, obviously shoppers returning from Monte, but Susan was not amongst them. It was then that he realised she had not come on the bus at all and was not, in fact, going to turn up this afternoon.

His interest in the class promptly died and,

205

as if ashamed of the fact, he returned to the task of preparing the clay with an additional spurt of concentration. But he had to admit, in a secret corner of his mind, that without Susan's companionship he wasn't going to enjoy himself. The children interested him so long as they behaved themselves; when they did not, his patience wore thin. At such moments it was Susan who took control and he was not only thankful for her, but delighted by her. In such a way, he had dreamed, would she mother her own children some day. His children. Their children.

Although his natural optimism had asserted itself since their last meeting and, characteristically, he had refused to be troubled by her rejection, a flicker of doubt now entered his mind. If she was staying away because she didn't want to see him, perhaps she was actually going to prove more obstinate than he anticipated. Self-doubt had never been part of Pierre's character and the fact that Susan might actually mean what she said about not marrying him had not troubled him for long.

This fellow she declared she was in love with, this Englishman to whom she meant nothing—what sort of a rival was he? A girl would grow tired of unreciprocated love—of that Pierre was confident. And when she did, she would accept more willingly the love which was waiting for her. Susan would grow weary of pining for something she could not have—and the sooner that happened, the better, he thought truculently.

Annoyance flicked his mind with an irritating gesture. It was unfair of her to let him down like this, leaving him with a class of obstreperous children to cope with single-handed. The fact that the class consisted of a mere handful and that, for the most part, these convalescent children were too apathetic to be obstreperous was one he completely overlooked. Susan had deserted him and he was resentful and angry. So much so that a petulant frown creased his handsome forehead and when Catherine shepherded the children into the playroom she observed his expression with some surprise.

Pierre was an amiable youth—or so she had always thought. In fact, he was rather charming. His obvious devotion to Susan had pleased her, rather than annoyed, because she was all in favour of the girl being paired off with someone of her own age. Even in her present state of mixed emotions, of fear and confusion and determination, Catherine still wanted John's devotion exclusively for herself. She refused to acknowledge that her own feelings had in any way changed.

Catherine dismissed Pierre from her mind because she had problems of her own. All-absorbing problems. Chief amongst them was the decision she had come to regarding Diana

Beaumont's proffered donation to the clinic. In the cold light of reasoning she knew this decision to be not only dishonest, but the most arrant folly. Nevertheless, there seemed no other alternative; no other way out. Stephen Foster had been in touch with her again, telephoning whilst she was in the ward kitchen this morning and using a tone which was no longer suave, but threatening. Fortunately, there had been no one in the office to answer the phone and she had answered it herself on the extension. Fortunately, also, the junior nurse, whom she was instructing in the preparation of diet trays, understood very little English, so her own side of the conversation—restrained as she could possibly make it—meant nothing to the girl.

But it had left an intensity of fear in Catherine's heart, doubling her sense of urgency and clinching once and for all her determination to go through with this final action. She paused no longer to consider the folly of it. There was no other way out; no other method to choose. It was the last, desperate gamble—and surely it couldn't fail?

Diana Beaumont was coming this afternoon. Catherine herself had fixed the time to coincide with John's session in the laboratory. And it wouldn't take long. The interview would soon be over and the cheque in her possession. Meanwhile, she mustn't pause to think or to falter.

She was settling the children at the long table when she heard Pierre's voice ask sullenly: 'And where is Suzanne, Madame? She has let me down this afternoon.'

He was lifting a little girl on to a high chair and automatically rolling some clay for her, but his mind was not on the task.

'Didn't you know, Pierre? She's left the clinic. She isn't coming back.'

'*What!* When did this happen?'

'She gave her notice last time she came, and left the same day.'

'But why, Madame? And why she not tell me? I take her home that day, but she say nothing. Nothing at all!'

'Perhaps she forgot,' Catherine said weakly.

'Forgot! *Mais non*, she keep silent deliberately—I see that now. And why? I tell you why! Because she know that if *she* leave, *I* leave, Madame. And so I shall!'

'That would be a pity,' John's voice cut in. 'The children have benefited so much from your classes.'

Pierre spun round. John was standing at the door and now, closing it behind him, he came across the room. The children shouted greetings, some climbing down from their chairs and rushing to meet him.

Pierre ran a harassed hand through his hair and said wildly: 'You see? How can I manage them alone? First I seat them at the table and then they are down, clambering all over the place! *C'est impossible, M'sieu!* Without Suzanne, I cannot take this class!'

John and Catherine were getting the children back into their places—John showing no sign of the anxiety he felt. He did not underrate the value of this occupational therapy and the thought of its loss disturbed him. He had come along to discuss with Pierre the possibility of engaging someone else to help him.

'I thought there might be a local person, or even one of your workers who might be released for an hour?' he suggested. 'It would mean extra employment for them and I should value their services.'

Pierre shrugged helplessly.

'I know no one—no one. As for my workers, they are needed at the pottery in my absence.'

'Of course. Then we must delegate a member of the staff.' John looked at Catherine hopefully. 'Could you help, Nurse? You have excellent control over the children and the class only lasts half-an-hour.'

'Not today!' she said quickly. 'I'm coaching Nurse Dubois and Nurse Le Fevre, and since they are both supposed to be off duty and I've had the hardest job in the world to persuade them to give an hour of it to study, I simply can't forego it!'

'Then we must release a junior nurse from the infants' ward.'

'There is only one on duty at this hour. Only

one is needed whilst they sleep.'

'Then tell one of the nurses from another ward to keep an eye on them,' John said a trifle impatiently. 'It's for a very short time, after all!'

'Very well,' said Catherine, and turned to the door.

Pierre burst out angrily: 'It is because of that man that Suzanne do this to me! That Englishman she is in love with!'

There was a stony little silence, broken only by the activity of the children who, oblivious of the adult discussion going on about them, delighted in the opportunity to slap their clay around without guidance.

Catherine's hand was arrested upon the door knob. John stared at the boy.

'What Englishman?' he asked quietly.

'The handsome one staying at the Villa d'Este, of course! I meet him the other day. "She means nothing to me!" he say—and so, of course, I know he must be the man Suzanne tells me about! And why? Because she admit this man she loves is not aware of her. "I mean nothing to him!" she say. "Nothing at all, Pierre!" Of course, the man is a fool and blind, but what is that to me? Now I must stand by and wait for her to realise that she waste her time—*and* my devotion! For a long time it has been taken for granted that one day Suzanne and I shall marry!'

John said levelly: 'What is the man's name?'

'Ferguson,' Pierre answered sulkily. 'Simon Ferguson, I understand.'

'The man who telephoned her one day,' John said, half to himself. 'I remember. I didn't like his voice . . .'

'Nor do I like *him*, M'sieu! He is too charming, too handsome with his shining blond hair and his smooth manners and oh, so amiable smile!'

John's glance became more intent. Catherine's hand turned the door knob quietly. She was halfway out of the room when she heard his voice say:

'Is he tall, this man?'

'Very tall, M'sieu. You know him, perhaps? You recognise the description, I see. Then you know he is no good, this M'sieu Ferguson, and his attentions to Suzanne are not desirable. And yet she go with him to the Sporting Club the other night—she tell me so!'

Catherine closed the door and hurried down the corridor. She felt sick and frightened, pursued by a sense of urgency more intense than she had ever known. To anyone who had met him, there was no mistaking that description of Stephen Foster, and although John had no reason to suspect the man's presence in Monte Carlo, he might well be curious. He might even decide to find out for himself.

Deliberately, she shut her mind to fear. Panic could only distort reason and at all costs she had to think clearly. She must also act swiftly. For the last time, Stephen must be persuaded to go away—right away—so that if John took it into his head to call at the Villa d'Este, he wouldn't find him.

She took a deep and steadying breath. John wasn't likely to leave the clinic until he had finished his work for the day; there was an accumulation of work in the laboratory—he had told her so this morning, adding that he didn't wish to be interrupted this afternoon until it was completed. There were x-rays to be developed, a task he was continuing to do himself until a qualified person could be employed. There was a test meal to be analysed and a blood count to be checked. These were important tasks which he was not likely to put on one side. Besides, he was a doctor first, last and foremost, so she knew she could rely on him not to let personal issues interfere.

Besides—why should he? Curiosity could be his only reason for deciding to investigate the identity of this Simon Ferguson. And why should he even be tempted to? He had never thought much of Stephen Foster and had said on more than one occasion that he never wished to see the man again. Catherine decided thankfully that she was letting imagination and fear run away with common sense.

All the same, there was no time to be lost.

She glanced at her watch and saw that Diana Beaumont was already overdue—or perhaps she had arrived and was already waiting in the office?

A glance out of the window confirmed this. Diana's luxurious car was parked in the drive.

Catherine opened the office door briskly, extending her hand with a charming smile, and was gratified when the woman seized it in both of hers and said without any preliminary: 'My dear, I'm so glad you sent for me—so glad of your decision! I knew you would agree, of course, because I knew you had the welfare of the clinic at heart.'

Catherine had the grace to feel ashamed. She looked away swiftly, inwardly vowing that once this was done she would start afresh, living her life as it ought to be lived; she would finish with lies and deceit and pretence.

'How much do you think the clinic could do with, Nurse?'

Catherine achieved a laugh.

'Well, as to that, any hospital or clinical organisation can never have enough funds! It is up to you to donate what you wish to donate.'

'Very well—although no amount could really match up to my gratitude to Doctor Curtis. Shall I give you the cheque now or leave it until Sally goes home?'

Catherine's hands clenched convulsively. Not that! she thought. No postponement, for goodness sake! Stephen wouldn't wait—he'd told her that, and he meant it. 'I'll give you until the week-end, my dear—by which time my hotel bill will be due and, of course, a man has to have more than one week's funds to keep him going.'

The week-end was only four days hence. If she paid that cheque into the bank today, there'd be just time to clear it. Meanwhile, she would have to see him—or reach him by phone, to assure him the matter was dealt with and to command him, *implore* him if necessary, to keep out of sight until the cash came through.

She was surprised to hear how steady her voice was as she answered: 'Just as you like— although, of course, constant financial demands are inevitable in a place like this—'

'You mean it would help to have it now? What about the endorsement, Nurse? Doctor Curtis will have to sign it, won't he?'

'Only if you make it out to him personally. He has made arrangements with the Bank for either one of us—my husband, or myself—to endorse cheques made out to the clinic . . .' *(And to cash them, too, thank God!)* 'It saves time in an organisation which has no secretary—'

Diana Beaumont was writing briskly. As she did so she remarked conversationally: 'I thought I'd seen a rather attractive little secretary here?'

215

'Only part-time. She comes to work on the manuscript of John's book—not to do the office work. John has been attending to that himself, but now all three of us share it. It simplifies things.'

Diana signed the cheque with a flourish, tore it from the hook, and handed it over.

Folded within the pocket of Catherine's crisp uniform, the slip of paper felt like a reprieve.

CHAPTER TWENTY

It was at that precise moment that Charlotte arrived. She had come deliberately. Normally she came to the clinic whenever she had completed a pile of mending, or on laundry days to check things in the linen room, but this afternoon she brought merely a bundle of children's socks. This didn't escape Catherine's eye and her brows lifted in surprise.

'How very conscientious of you, Mrs. Fothergill, to come all the way from Monte Carlo with such a small parcel!'

And why, said her glance, was it necessary to bring it here—to the office?

Charlotte was quite unpefturbed.

'Oh, I didn't come especially to deliver these—the children have plenty to go on with; I know. I merely thought I'd bring them at the same time that I came to see Doctor Curtis.'

'Is he expecting you?'

'No.'

'Then I'm afraid he'll be too busy to see you, Mrs. Fothergill.'

'Then I'll wait.'

Catherine's shoulders lifted in a faint shrug.

'Very well. I'll tell him you're waiting in the linen room.'

'Thank you, but I'll wait here. I won't be disturbing anyone, since Susan isn't working here any more. Has Doctor Curtis engaged the full-time secretary you told her he was getting, Nurse?'

Could it be alarm which flashed in Catherine's eyes? It was hard to tell, for this young woman was expert at hiding her feelings. At hiding a great many things, thought Charlotte sagely.

Diana Beaumont was putting on her gloves, smiling at the old lady as she did so.

'Has that nice young secretary left, then? What a pity—I thought she was charming and that Doctor Curtis obviously thought a lot of her.'

'He certainly did,' Charlotte answered significantly.

'Couldn't she be persuaded to remain?'

Catherine put in quickly: 'John needs someone full-time. The clinic is growing rapidly.'

'I'm glad to hear it. Well, goodbye, Nurse—

217

you'll pay that cheque in for me, won't you?'

'Of course!'

Catherine was aware of Charlotte's alert glance and disliked her, at that moment, more than she had ever done. She rallied swiftly, however. The fact that the old lady heard Diana mention a cheque was no cause for alarm, preferable as it would have been that no one but herself should know about it.

To her relief, Charlotte said: 'I'll just put these socks away, Nurse,' and left them.

Catherine saw Diana off the premises and then went to the staff sitting-room. It was empty—as she had known it would be at this hour. She was in a hurry to examine the cheque, knowing it would be a generous one and more than ample for her needs. And, after all, it would only be a loan—she'd pay it back, bit by bit, and pray that John would never find out. Unfortunately, it had to be made out to the clinic, which meant that the original sum would be entered into the bank account and the amount of her withdrawals, also, but she would think up some explanation for those. Fortunately, he had entrusted her with the ordering of medical supplies and why shouldn't she pay for them in cash? That could be a temporary explanation, at least.

In any case, all that was in the future—and, if her luck held, there need be no questions or explanations. Week by week she would replace the money, entering the payments in the books as small receipts from various sources—oh, she'd think of something! She always thought of something!

She stood with the cheque in her hand, astonishment and relief surging through her in a warm tide. Diana Beaumont had been generous indeed! In this unguarded moment all Catherine's thoughts were mirrored in her face as nakedly as a film upon a screen. There was no one to see her; she was alone, and safe ... She closed her eyes in an ecstasy of relief.

'I shouldn't do it, if I were you,' said a voice gently.

Catherine's eyes flew open. She whirled round and saw Charlotte watching her from the door. She thrust the cheque back into her pocket and Charlotte came into the room, shutting the door quietly behind her.

'Don't do it, my dear,' she said kindly. 'Nothing can be worth such a step.'

'I—I don't know what you mean! And what are you doing here, may I ask?'

'Looking for you. When I went back to the office you weren't there. I knew you'd gone to see Sally's mother off, and that you'd want to be alone after she had gone—I guessed that. So the only other place you were likely to be was here—unless you'd gone upstairs to your flat, and I didn't think that likely when you were on call ...'

'Get out of here! Do you hear me? Get out!'

'But this is the staff sitting-room, which

219

means that even as a part-time member I am entitled to be here!'

Catherine strode towards the door. Charlotte immediately barred her path.

'Tell me I'm an interfering old busybody and I'll agree with you, but it won't prevent me from interfering nevertheless. Unless you promise not to do what I think you are planning to do, I shall tell your husband, Mrs. Collier.'

'*You wouldn't dare!*'

'Oh, yes, I would—and not merely for his sake, nor for the sake of the clinic, but even for you, you silly girl. You've been giving in to Stephen Foster, haven't you? I think you've been doing it long enough.'

Catherine gasped: '*How do you know he is Stephen Foster?*'

'English newspapers publish overseas editions, my dear—ever thought of that? I recognised the man who calls himself Ferguson from the photographs of Doctor Foster, published in the press. Why are you afraid of him, Mrs. Collier?'

Her voice was kind—unbelievably and quite genuinely kind. Catherine felt a desperate weeping rise up from her heart and it was the kindness in this woman's voice which caused it.

Oh, dear God! she thought hopelessly. *None of it has been any use because this woman has known all along! She's guessed . . . and now I can hide nothing!*

With the realisation came despair.

'Leave me alone,' she said dully. 'Leave me alone—please!'

'I will, when I've helped you—'

'Helped me! *You*? Why should you help me?'

'Because, in return, you're going to do something to help Susan. You're going to tell John Curtis exactly why Susan left him.'

'No ! No, I can't!'

'For a woman who has submitted to Stephen Foster these past weeks, you are showing a singular lack of courage when it comes to taking a step which, by comparison, should be practically painless.'

'I won't do it! I—I *couldn't* tell him!'

'You couldn't tell him that you lied to Susan to get her out of the way? You couldn't tell him that you knew he had fallen in love with her and that you hated her for it? Very well. Then *I* will tell your husband that Stephen Foster is at the Villa d'Este, why I believe he came here, and why he has remained . . . *and* what you plan to do with the cheque Diana Beaumont gave you. Why did she give it to you, by the way?'

'Merely as advance payment of Sally's account—'

'I don't believe that. I know accounts aren't normally rendered until treatment is complete. Anyway, it doesn't matter. The fact remains that to do what you were planning to do, when

221

I came in just now, would be more than foolhardy. It would be criminal.'

'I was only going to *borrow*—' Catherine sobbed.

It was then that she broke down. With infinite pity, Charlotte took hold of her shoulders and the sound of Catherine's weeping filled the silent room.

Walking down the passage outside, Peter heard and recognised the sound, for he had occasionally heard such weeping in the night, although he had never let Catherine know.

He opened the door.

'Catherine—'

His wife's head jerked up. Charlotte's hands fell from her shoulders.

'What's going on here?' Peter looked from one to the other.

Charlotte urged gently: 'Tell him, Catherine—tell him everything.'

'No, no! I can't—*I can't!*'

Peter looked at her for a long moment. Charlotte crossed to the door and left them alone.

Peter said: 'Look at me, Catherine.'

There was a new note in his voice, a note of authority which she instinctively obeyed.

'What was it Charlotte told you to tell me?'

Suddenly, she knew that she had lost. And in that moment she knew why it hurt so desperately and why she had really given into Stephen Foster these past weeks.

Peter saw the despair in her eyes and heard the resignation in her voice as she answered: 'If you go to the Villa d'Este, you'll find Stephen Foster there. He has a note—the last of several—which I wrote to him some time ago. The others I've bought from him—and destroyed.'

She didn't look at him. She stood rigid and numb as the silence grew between them. Then Peter asked unemotionally: 'Was it important to you, Catherine—your *affaire* with him, I mean? I often wondered.'

She stared at him for a long and incredulous moment.

'You knew?'

'Of course. What I didn't know was what it meant to you. I didn't believe you were in love with him, so I put it down to the unsatisfactory life we were leading. I resolved to break with him, then things happened which broke up the partnership anyway . . .' He looked at her searchingly, then repeated: *'Was* it serious, Catherine?'

'No,' she answered truthfully. 'It was never serious. But it—amused me—and helped to ease the boredom I felt in those days. But the notes could have been misunderstood.'

'And you thought I, in particular, would misunderstand them, if I saw them?'

'Yes. In fact I thought it was what everyone would do. Not only you, but John. Solicitors, too, if it came to the point. Besides, Stephen

223

threatened to ruin the clinic by spreading scandal . . .'

'What possible scandal could he spread?'

'That John's wrist was injured whilst operating in an unfit condition. You and I know that isn't true, but others wouldn't. There's the scar to prove it—and the fact that he gave up surgery to come here—'

'Plus the fact that Foster, not John, was dismissed from the hospital, proof of which could easily be obtained! My dear girl, didn't you think of that? It wasn't even *necessary* to give in to him!'

A long shudder ran through her.

'I was too terrified to realise that—so terrified I couldn't think clearly.' She gave a long sigh and turned away from him. 'Well— now you know, Peter. You know everything.'

'I only know that to drive you to such desperate steps the fear of what I might do must have been pretty terrible!'

'It was.'

'So I must mean something to you, after all . . .'

'*Mean* something!' she cried. 'Oh, Peter, just how much I didn't know myself until now!'

His arms went about her. He held her close. She clung to him desperately and cried: 'I don't deserve a man like you, Peter! Why don't you tell me to go? Why haven't you left me long before this?'

'Because I love you—for better, or for

worse. And from now on it's going to be for better, Catherine, or you'll *really* have me to reckon with. We'll make a good job of our marriage and we'll start by shouldering a bit of responsibility—parental responsibility. We'll have a family, whether you like the idea or not, and we'll make a good job of that, too!'

'We will,' she promised soberly. 'We really will, Peter . . .'

The shrill peal of the telephone cut into the moment. Peter answered it. The conversation was brief, then he replaced the receiver and looked at her.

'That was Diana Beaumont. She said she was ringing back to let you know that she post-dated the cheque because she'll have to arrange with her bank to transfer the necessary funds from England, and that will take a bit of time. She said she meant to tell you and then Mrs. Fothergill interrupted and she forgot. What cheque was she talking about?'

Catherine took the piece of paper from her pocket, stared at it, and began to laugh. The laughter finished up on a note of hysteria. Peter took hold of her shoulders and shook her, hard.

The laughter ceased abruptly. She looked at her husband and thought soberly: 'You don't know, you'll *never* know, what a narrow escape I've had . . .'

Aloud, she said: 'She gave me a donation for the clinic. Persuade John to accept it, will

225

you, Peter?'

She put the cheque into his hands.

'Later, my dear. I've something more urgent to attend to right now.'

He moved purposefully towards her and took her in his arms again.

After a while, Catherine stirred. There was something she had to do. It wouldn't be pleasant, it wouldn't be easy, but she knew, now, that she could face it.

'I have to find John,' she said.

'And I have work to do!'

Peter kissed her and for a moment she clung to him, pressing her cheek against his. 'Don't worry about Stephen Foster,' he said softly. 'If the fellow turns up again, *I'll* deal with him. As for you and me, Catherine, this is a new beginning.'

'A new beginning,' she echoed sincerely, and watched him as he returned to the wards. There was something about his step—something confident and happy—which she had never seen before. Her own, too, felt lighter as she walked down the corridor to John's laboratory.

In the distance, she saw Charlotte coming towards her, but, before they met, the laboratory door opened and John emerged. A detached part of Catherine's mind noted that he had shed his white overall. In one hand he held a batch of x-rays.

'Ah—there you are, Nurse. I was coming to

look for you.' He addressed her in an impersonal, professional tone which, she realised, had become habitual of late. A sense of loss touched her heart briefly, then was gone. And in that moment she acknowledged that everything between herself and John had been over for a long time. She alone had clung to it, stubbornly and vainly, because she could not bear the thought of losing any man's devotion.

He held out the plates. 'Pass these on to Peter, will you? He'll be waiting for them. And if you've come for that blood-count, it's ready in the lab. The test-meal, too.'

'You've worked quickly—'

'I've had to. There's something I've got to attend to, urgently.'

He gave her a brief nod and turned to go. She knew that he had forgotten her.

'John! I want to talk to you—'

He turned impatiently.

'What is it, Catherine? Can't it wait? I'm in a hurry—'

'It's about Susan!'

His attention was immediate.

'What about Susan?' he demanded, and the taut note in his voice didn't escape her either.

Catherine took a deep breath.

'I think you should know why she *really* left. She believed you were engaging another secretary in her place.'

'She thought *that*? But how could she? Who

told her such a thing?'

Charlotte's voice cut in: 'Why—I did, Doctor! Did I make a mistake? I'm so very sorry, but wasn't that what you said in the office—that you'd have to engage a full-time secretary now the clinic was growing?' Her wrinkled face surveyed him in penitent concern. 'Oh, dear—if I said the wrong thing, you must forgive me!'

'Forgive you?' he cried furiously. 'Charlotte, I could shake you! I could do worse than that! Do you realise what you've done?'

'*John*—' Catherine put in swiftly, but Charlotte's restraining hand took hold of her arm.

It was too late, anyway—John was striding down the corridor; racing down the stairs. They heard the thud of the front door and his footsteps hurrying across the gravel drive towards his car. A moment later the engine revved urgently, gathered speed, then disappeared into the distance.

'He has gone to Susan,' Catherine said quietly.

'I hope so, my dear. I hope so, indeed.'

'You shouldn't have stopped me from telling him the truth, Charlotte. Why did you?'

'Haven't you done enough confessing for one day, my dear?'

The kindly old face smiled gently. Catherine reached out spontaneously and kissed the wrinkled cheek.

'You meant it kindly, but it was a waste of time, Charlotte—he's bound to learn who really told Susan that he . . .'

'And by that time,' Charlotte reassured her comfortingly, 'it won't matter—not even to you.'

'But in the meantime, it is you he will blame.'

'Not for long. He'll forgive an old woman—especially when he sets eyes on Susan again . . .'

John did that sooner than he expected. She was sitting at the reception desk when he entered the Villa d'Este and for a moment they stared at one another without speaking.

He said gruffly: 'So you're not working at the British Consulate, after all.'

'I start tomorrow.'

'We'll see about that.'

Her proud little chin tilted.

'I beg your pardon?'

'I said, we'll see about that!' His voice echoed forcefully in the quiet room which, mercifully, was empty. A moment later he was reaching across the desk and pulling her to her feet. 'I want to talk to you, Susan, but I'm damned if I'm going to do so across anything so impersonal as an office desk! Come over here.'

He thrust her unceremoniously into an armchair and sat down opposite her. She was so stunned that she obeyed without protest.

'There are one or two things to be cleared

229

up,' he said deliberately, 'and you're going to listen to me without interrupting. Understand?'

She nodded her head in a dazed fashion.

'First, it was totally and absolutely untrue that I ever contemplated engaging another secretary. It was *you* I wanted, Susan. I intended to ask you to come full-time—but I admit I've changed my mind about that now.'

A light went out of her eyes.

'Oh—you have?'

'I most definitely have.' His strong face, serious and unsmiling, surveyed her sternly. 'Secondly, I want to know the identity of this Englishman you're in love with.'

For a moment, she sat very still.

'Who told you?' she whispered. 'Pierre?'

'I'm grateful to him. I'm even grateful for his description of the man.'

Susan interrupted in surprise: 'He— *described* him? But how could he?'

'Very vividly indeed. I recognised the man at once, no matter what name he happens to be parading under. Which brings me to my real reason for being here. I want to see this Simon Ferguson.'

A dimple quivered at the corner of her mouth, so fleetingly that he wondered if he had actually seen it.

John leaned forward and took both her hands in his. The sternness went from his voice.

'Susan, you're very young—perhaps you

230

don't like to be told that, but it's true. You're also unsophisticated and trusting, and, God knows, I wouldn't have you any different, but it's because of these qualities that I want to protect you from men like Stephen Foster. That is his real name, by the way.'

'I know.'

'You—what?'

'I said I know.' Again the dimple quivered beside her mouth, but this time it remained. 'You seem surprised, Doctor Curtis . . .'

'John,' he corrected automatically, 'and I am surprised.'

'Why? Because, as you say, I'm young and trusting and unsophisticated? That may be true, but I'm not a fool, Doctor Curtis—I mean, John—and when a man starts slandering another and making up stories which can't possibly be true—'

His mouth tightened.

'What sort of stories?'

Her glance went to his wrist. She said slowly: 'About surgeons operating when unfit to . . .' Her eyes lifted, and met his. 'Trusting, did you call me? I don't trust people who suggest things so completely out of character that I know they can't be true.'

'Did he tell you that—about me?'

'He tried to. But not for long.' Her voice trembled—so did her hands within his own. 'I knew, then, that he was a dangerous man, not to be believed.'

'And yet, you fell in love with him.'

'It was Pierre who said that. Not I.'

His hands tightened upon hers and she said swiftly: 'It was he—Stephen Foster—who bungled that operation, wasn't it, John? And you tried to stop him.'

'He didn't get a chance to bungle it, my dear—I *did* stop him. Unfortunately—this—was the result.' He half-turned his wrist, not releasing his grasp. 'But that's all in the past, and no matter what tale he tries to spread around, or for what motive, the truth can always be substantiated. Peter witnessed the operation. Catherine was on theatre duty, too.'

'Catherine?' There was a new note of enquiry in her voice; an anxious note. For a long moment they looked at one another and then, briefly, he nodded. 'Yes—I was in love with her. Long ago. How did you guess?'

'I didn't. She told me, once, that you were important to each other—'

'But not any more.'

'I'm glad,' she answered quietly.

'Why? Does it matter to you, Susan?'

A lovely colour flooded her cheeks, but she made no answer.

John said: 'I must see Foster—at once.'

'I'm afraid you can't. He's gone.'

'Gone!'

'Mother sent him packing. This morning. She showed him the newspaper cuttings Charlotte had given her, and asked why he had

232

registered under another name. His past, she said, hadn't anything to do with her—but the present had, and she wouldn't have anyone staying in her hotel under false pretences. He was—rather disconcerted.'

'I can imagine!' John said grimly. 'He won't come back, more's the pity. I'd like to deal with the man myself. I may be wrong, but I think he's been in touch with Catherine. He telephoned her one day and I recognised his voice as the man who also telephoned you.' He broke off and regarded her jealously. 'Pierre tells me you went to the Sporting Club with him one night.'

'That's true. I enjoyed myself, too. He was very charming.'

The dimple beside her mouth, John decided, was the most maddening and the most delightful thing about her.

'Pierre also told me—'

There was a sound behind them. John swore heartily and turned to see Pierre standing just within the front door.

'Suzanne—'

'Come here, Pierre!' she ordered severely.

He obeyed, looking sheepish.

'Suzanne, *ma petite*, I come to ask forgiveness—'

'I should think so, too! What made you tell Doctor Curtis that I was in love with that man?'

Pierre's penitence disappeared. He was

indignant, protesting, voluble.

'You tell me so, Suzanne! You tell me so yourself. But, yes—you cannot deny! You say you love an Englishman who does not return your love; a fool of a man to whom you mean nothing! It is true, is it not? See—you do not deny it, even now—!'

He broke off, staring at the pair of them; at Susan's flushed and embarrassed face; at her eyes, gazing at John Curtis with a sudden and expressive shyness; at the doctor himself, standing rooted to the spot and staring back at her in questioning disbelief.

They appeared to have forgotten him. The world seemed to have dropped away, leaving them in exquisite isolation, so intensely aware of one another that even he was silenced; even he, who thought he knew what love was and who now discovered that he had only known a boy-and-girl affection.

He smiled, shrugged philosophically and went away. Someday he, too, would find what Suzanne had found. Someday he, too, would come face to face with the enchantment which that reserved Englishman was experiencing now.

It was Susan who first realised they were alone again. She took a stern hold upon herself and said: 'So you don't want me back? You won't employ me as your secretary? You've changed your mind about asking me to work full-time?'

John came to life instantly.

'I most certainly have!' he declared, and in one swift movement gathered her close. 'Of course, I don't want you as my secretary! When you come back to St. Maria it will be as my wife—*my wife*, understand?' And to silence any protests his mouth came down upon hers.

Not, of course, that Susan had the slightest protest to make.

We hope you have enjoyed this Large Print book. Other Chivers Press or G.K. Hall & Co. Large Print books are available at your library or directly from the publishers.

For more information about current and forthcoming titles, please call or write, without obligation, to:

Chivers Press Limited
Windsor Bridge Road
Bath BA2 3AX
England
Tel. (01225) 335336

OR

G.K. Hall & Co.
P.O. Box 159
Thorndike, Maine 04986
USA
Tel. (800) 223-2336

All our Large Print titles are designed for easy reading, and all our books are made to last.